Searching for Proof and Faith

by

Waverly Hasty Cowart
and Richard Hasty

Searching for Proof and Faith

Edition #2

by Waverly Hasty Cowart and Richard Hasty

Unless otherwise noted, all scriptural references are taken from the Bible, English Standard Version, © 2001 by Crossway, a publishing ministry of Good News Publishers

This book has been updated and revised from the previously published work of the same name, © 2012 by SPF100 ASIN: B008R311BY

Cover art by Kolapo Olanrewaju of Soul Sonshine

Interior design by Susan Louise Gabriel of Soul Sonshine

ISBN-13: 978-1-960982-04-9

Published by Soul Sonshine, LLC
P.O. Box 914
Springtown, TX 76082

Dedication

"…we will tell the next generation the praiseworthy deeds of the Lord, his power, and the wonders he has done."

(Psalm 78:4)

This book is dedicated to the next generation— that they might know our Creator's great wonders, and come to know Him personally.

Acknowledgements

As is so often the case, there are far too many people who have contributed to the content and inspiration for this revision than can be mentioned! But we want to at least thank a few while hoping the many others will forgive us for having too little space to mention their names.

Thank you, Susan Gabriel and Soul Sonshine for guiding us through this rewrite process.

Thank you to Josiah, an acknowledged skeptic, for sharing your questions and challenges!

We really appreciated the continued encouragement of Bill, Joel, and Andy who've offered constant thinking on topics, and Grace Fellowship Church, an inspiring community.

But we would be most remiss not to remember Norm Geisler and his thoughtful and loving approach to defending the gospel throughout his lifetime. May we too be so faithful to the end.

Table of Contents

About the Authors

Waverly Hasty Cowart graduated in 2008 with a degree in English from the University of North Carolina at Chapel Hill, where she was a Young Life leader and an Alpha Delta Pi sorority member. She also has a Master's in Christian Counseling from Gordon-Conwell Theological Seminary. Today she is married to Daniel and the mother of three beautiful children.

(waverlyhcowart@gmail.com)

Richard Hasty is a former Board Member at Southern Evangelical Seminary and the founder of Leave.Now.Grow Consulting, focused on equipping leaders to develop other leaders. He and Shereé, his wife of more than forty years, have three children and nine grandchildren. They live in Charlotte, North Carolina.

(RHasty@LeaveNowGrow.com)

Foreword

By Norman L. Geisler

Soon after I became a Christian, it was very clear to me how important it was to be able to defend my faith. That awareness inspired me to spend the last fifty years studying and teaching others how to grow their faith and debate the issues of Christianity. I have become even more determined over the years to build knowledge and confidence in young people so that they may share their faith and stand strong in the face of the onslaught of a post-modern world – a society that not only avoids a Christian label but has become increasingly hostile toward those of us who have given our lives to Christ.

Most high school students cannot possibly anticipate the pressure they will be under to conform to the views of their professors and peers in college — especially if they will be attending a secular university. If they have not learned how to defend their position on the critical tenets of Christianity, then their ability to hold onto their faith will be severely and unnecessarily weakened in the days ahead.

A recent Barna survey informs us that 92% of our evangelical Christian young people do not even understand a Christian worldview,[1] let alone know how to defend it. This was brought home with great force when we were informed by the leaders of a church at which we were scheduled to speak, that their top youth leader had just converted to Islam!

She and most of the people at the Mosque she attended came to our meeting to witness to her former Christian friends to win them to Islam.

We desperately need to teach our youth about the reasonable evidence behind our faith. Whether they attend religious schools, home-schools, or public schools they are being bombarded one way or another with a non-Christian worldview. Every day, our students are influenced by a society that leads them to believe that our faith in Christ is based on myths and irrational beliefs. If we fail to meet this challenge head-on, then our young people will continue to leave our churches at an alarming 75% rate. That's right, surveys show that three out of four evangelical youth reject the Christian faith while they are in college!

Searching for Proof and Faith brings a fresh perspective to young people, not only creatively introducing the arguments for Christianity, but also helping to equip high school and college students to respond appropriately to others who have questions or challenges to the Christian faith. This book also provides an excellent bibliography of resources and a great context for discussion, using a unique story-like approach that will elevate the interest of both Christians and non-Christians alike.

Dr. Norman Geisler passed away in 2019, just shy of his 87th birthday. He is one of the most prolific theological and apologetics authors of the 20th and 21st centuries. As such, he has spoken or debated in all fifty states and in twenty-five countries. He is the author or co-author of more than 100 books, yet never shied away from even the simplest of conversations on the topics that were the foundation of his faith in Christ.

Preface

While now is the time to revise our original book, we can't help but remember the original motivation to write a simple and easy-to-read introduction to apologetics. We were compelled by a desire to help teenagers and others begin to explore the critical foundations of Christianity that are so commonly attacked today. Are these foundations reliable or just built on fables easily dispelled by modern science and culture? Paul says in Romans 1:18:

> ...since the creation of the world God's invisible qualities
> – his eternal power and divine nature – have been clearly
> seen, being understood from what has been made, so
> that men are without excuse. *(NIV)*

So why, as Dr. Geisler states, are 92% of evangelical students unable to defend their faith? Where are "God's invisible qualities" revealed, if not in the Bible?

Our original investigation into apologetics was a weekly study that grew to more than ten high school students. First, to search for the evidence of God that existed outside of the Bible, and later to pursue a faith that is revealed in the most historically accurate and reliable book known to mankind.

During our time together, the students asked questions, and we would explore logical, scientific, and philosophically sound answers together. Each time God's wisdom was revealed, even without using the Book that is often maligned by those who don't recognize its origin — or their own.

Searching for Proof and Faith is the result of our research into the works of Norman Geisler, Frank Turek, Lee Strobel, Rebecca McLaughlin, Josh McDowell, Alisa Childers, Hugh Ross, Michael Behe, and many others. Through their own scholarship and commitment to sound research, they demonstrated that Christianity is not only defensible but is the only logical answer to life's most penetrating questions.

In the end, we recognize that no evidence will be enough for those who don't want to believe. Ultimately, it's the will that prevents faith, not the mind, as evidence continues to mount that something, not nothing, created the universe we occupy today.

It is both humbling and fun to be a part of something that seems to be directed by One much bigger than yourself. Think of the feeling you get when you see the stars from the crystal clear view of a mountaintop; that is what it's like to experience a power so much bigger than yourself at work around you. We have witnessed His sovereignty in bringing together the ideas, the people, and events to make this book possible. May God be honored in the lives of those people who have contributed to this effort, and even more in those who take the time to read and explore the ideas in this book. We pray for each of our readers that it is just the beginning.

— Waverly Hasty Cowart and Richard Hasty

---

[1] Worldview is defined as: "The fundamental cognitive orientation of an individual or society encompassing the whole of the individual's or society's knowledge, culture, and point of view."
https://web.engr.oregonstate.edu/~funkk/Personal/worldview.html

—1—

Religion is for Uneducated People

"God is dead."

Harper Forshaw's first reaction was shock. She'd signed up for Philosophy 101 because she wanted to learn about logic and reasoning. She had long considered pursuing law school after undergrad and knew philosophy classes would be good preparation for it.

When the professor, Dr. Meek, opened class on the first day with this emphatic statement, she was baffled. She didn't expect to hear a lecture on religion.

Harper sat quietly like the rest of her freshman peers. A few were obviously uncomfortable and leaned back in their chairs. Others leaned forward, eager to hear his reasons for making such a bold statement.

"There is no credible evidence for god," he said, warming to the topic. "We must find divinity within ourselves, inspire our own lives, and improve the world around us."

Professor Meek urged his students to "make a difference in the world." He cited the work of the Peace Corps and the United Nations as examples of people making a difference. "Religion is just a lazy person's way to avoid solving real problems for real people," he concluded.

By the end of class that day, Harper's head was swimming with conflicting thoughts. Dr. Meek was enthusiastic and charmingly persuasive. He was very smart.

His logic seemed to be so, well… logical. But the statements he made so matter-of-factly crashed headlong into the Bible stories and sermons about God Harper had been raised on, the ones that she'd always believed were true.

By the middle of the semester, Harper's discomfort had evolved into respect and admiration as she listened with awe to her charismatic professor thoroughly and logically explain why believing in religious "dogma" was a silly waste of time.

She'd heard his attacks on religion so often and the way he argued them so persuasively, that she was now of the same mind — seemingly, along with the rest of his students.

Dr. Meek had several teaching assistants for his class of a hundred students. One of them was named Jayden Trotman. Jayden — Jay for short — was a tall, attractive junior who was majoring in philosophy and religion. Dr. Meek's respect for the young man was obvious, and he often allowed Jay to give short topical lectures during the last ten minutes of class. Jay appeared to be well on his way to maintaining a near-perfect GPA in his major.

Harper's feelings toward Jay were more than just respect; her interest in him grew every time she heard him speak with confidence and connect with the student audience. She was always part of the small group that lingered to ask questions on his topic after class. When he invited her to go for coffee after class one day to continue the intriguing discussion Dr. Meek had kickstarted in his lecture, Harper smiled with pleasure and accepted.

Jay, too, was convincing when he echoed Dr. Meek. "We

must find our own truth if we want to expand our minds and change the world," he told her.

Harper felt the weight of adulthood for the first time. She still felt a bit guilty for walking away from her beliefs about God, but she felt strongly that she needed to embrace the truth, not religious myths. Before college, the only religious studies she was familiar with were based on the Bible.

She thought back to the beginning of the semester. She'd been surprised to hear Dr. Meek and Jay declare so confidently that there was no way to prove God existed. She knew it was a perspective she'd never thought of before. But it was now almost mid-term, and she was considering the possibility that religious people were simply doing what they'd been taught by their parents.

She'd started to accept the idea that proof of God's existence was lacking. She also was beginning to see that perhaps her religious training was "fine for uneducated people, but not for really intelligent people."

She ignored the fact that her own parents were educated at Ivy League schools since that seemed to contradict her professor's insistence that "only uneducated people still believe in a real god."

That first semester, Harper also became acutely aware of the conflict between the scientific and religious views of how life came into existence. Professor Meek's words resonated in her head during her college biology class one day — "What is not logical, what cannot be proven, has no room in the educated mind."

In her Christian high school, the teacher had explained

Darwin's theory of natural selection but also asserted that the first few chapters of Genesis held the best explanation for the existence of the universe.

Her college biology professor, Dr. Stroud, however, soundly embarrassed her in front of the class when she asked him his view of the Biblical creation story.

"That's mythology for the naive! Is that what you want to be your whole life? Naive? Uninformed? Science is about what you can prove, not about faith. Study the truth, and leave mythology behind for children's story time.

"Now, for those of you who want to be serious students, let's get back to biology."

His words smarted. Harper had to choke down the lump in her throat as she turned away to hide her embarrassment. It had clearly been a miscalculation to bring up anything related to the Bible. She wouldn't make that mistake again with another professor at Blanchard.

But, she wanted to hear Jay's reaction to her experience, so she told him about it.

He responded reassuringly, "We all come to college with beliefs from our childhood, good and bad, and we all have stories our parents told us that aren't really true, like Santa Claus. After Dad left, Mom didn't have much time for church. And she sure didn't believe in somebody else's idea of a good god, so I didn't have to carry around that kind of baggage.

"Dr. Stroud didn't mean anything personal," Jay continued. "He was just making a point to open your mind beyond the childish ideas of Christianity — I hear he thinks of it as shock treatment for new students. But you're an adult now, Harper! You're in college, not grade school! It's time to think for yourself."

Later that week, Harper headed to the library to study for her biology midterm. She shuffled her feet through the leaves as she walked, remembering the many times she did the same while walking to class in high school.

"How quickly the semester has flown by," she thought. It seemed like only yesterday her parents and brother were helping her unpack in her tiny dorm room.

She had begged her parents to let her attend Blanchard University, a liberal arts college in a big city three hours from home. The desire to leave her small town behind and experience the world was a lure she couldn't resist.

Blanchard was certainly different from anything she had ever experienced before. By the end of the first week, the contrast between Blanchard and her Christian high school stood out sharply — *like night and day,* she thought.

She was determined to be an exceptional student at Blanchard. And her goal of maintaining the same high GPA she'd achieved at Covenant Academy often kept her in a quiet cubicle in the back of the library.

She found the biology coursework especially difficult. One of the assigned readings was about evolution:

> *All available evidence supports the central conclusions of evolutionary theory, that life on Earth has evolved over billions of years and all species share common ancestors.*

As she underlined the words, she started thinking about

the creation story taught in her Sunday School classes and reinforced in her grade school education. *If all the available evidence supports evolution, then the simple idea of God creating man must be another ignorant fable — one more way to control people's minds and keep them from thinking freely.*

"No one can prove that God created man. There's no evidence outside of the Bible." She was reminded of Jay's declaration that everything was randomly created by chance.

As she began taking notes on the article, Harper thought about how pleased Dr. Stroud would be with her insight.

Two hours later, Harper headed to Jay's dorm to discuss what she'd been studying. She'd just read the article Jay recommended to her. It was called "Epistemology: The True Theory of Knowledge." After reading that article, she concluded that church had been a wasteful part of her childhood.

Sitting cross-legged on the floor of Jay's dorm room, she listened attentively as he told her, "Going to church is just something people do until they go to college, you know? A silly phase that parents force on their kids. College is the place to expand your mind and embrace new truths. Religious people are so close-minded."

Jay reminisced. "Whenever my grandmother kept me, she always made me go to church. But once I became a teenager, she gave me a choice to go or not. It wasn't a hard choice for me. I left that god-stuff behind."

Jay was right. Harper appreciated his patience with her as she worked toward keeping her mind open to the new ideas presented both inside and outside her classes daily.

Then he sat on the floor close beside her and took her hand into both of his. He looked at her intently and said quietly, "My sweet Harper. You know I care for you and I wouldn't steer you in the wrong direction, don't you? There isn't any point in believing something with no evidence. And logically, it's impossible to prove there's a real God.

"It's actually kind of creepy thinking there's someone who watches everything you do and then condemns you if you do something wrong," he continued.

"I mean, I went to church once in a while until I was 15 and my dad left. My mom stopped making me go, and honestly, I just couldn't see a good reason to dress up, sing boring songs, and then have to sit and listen to someone telling me that I'm going to some place called 'hell' if I don't act right. I finally realized that hell is just another way to control simple-minded people because it doesn't fit logically with the rest of the stories about God.

"What kind of loving God would create hell, an eternal place of damnation? Not one I want to believe in! And when I got to Blanchard, I was able to explore my thoughts and engage with ideas without religion holding me back. I'm more of a free thinker now than I ever was before.

"And so are you!" he added emphatically.

"I know," Harper answered. "It's just hard sometimes for me to let go of something I believed in so strongly for so long. But I think I'm getting there."

She wanted to impress Jay with her "free" mind. She really liked him and was still occasionally amazed that she was dating someone like Jay — a junior teaching assistant and one of the most attractive guys at Blanchard — or, as she almost said out loud sometimes, *that he was dating her*!

Jay responded, "Don't take too long if you want to get away from that small town of yours. You need to let it go.

"Hey, let's go to the CowZone! I hear they're serving half-price smoothies and showing that Star Wars remake tonight! It will get your mind off religious fantasies for a while."

Jay felt proud of helping Harper become a free-thinking skeptic. He remembered the pain he felt when his dad left. He also remembered how often his dad spoke of church. *Some religious guy he was, leaving my mom and me with nothing. I made it this far by my own brain, not religion,* he thought to himself.

They headed toward the campus food court that was affectionately named after their school mascot, the Bulls and a spoof on their popular "we'll make it however you want it" Italian dish, calzone.

As they walked, Harper realized she didn't want to ruin the beginning of her relationship by letting Jay think she was close-minded or that she still felt a tug toward spiritual things.

But when Jay put his arm around her, Harper felt a different kind of tug.

A few weeks later, Harper felt like she was finally letting go of her "childhood fantasies" about God. But she had to avoid her mother's phone calls so she wouldn't have to lie about not going to church. Or the fact that she was looking into New Age religion.

Jay was now teaching her about self-spirituality, what he called "the god within you." They started meditating together every week as a way of relieving stress and getting in touch with their "inner selves."

Harper was relieved when she realized that this was an educated religion she could explain logically. But she still felt a twinge of guilt about hiding it from her parents.

Walking across campus one Tuesday, Harper heard someone call her name. She turned around to see the familiar face of Maya Thomas, a girl who had graduated a few years before her at Covenant High School. Maya was one of the people who'd encouraged Harper to apply to Blanchard.

Although they corresponded via email during the first few weeks of school, they were never able to find a convenient time to get together.

"Harper, you look great! How is your semester going?" Maya shouted with a big smile.

Preoccupation with her new boyfriend had caused Harper to forget that Maya was even at the same school until just now.

Harper tried to apologize. "It's going really well, actually. And I'm sorry we haven't gotten the chance to get together. I've just been so busy, and my classes have been so demanding…" she trailed off.

"I completely understand," Maya replied, smiling. "I remember how my first year went. I could barely find time to call my mom!"

Harper tried to laugh, shifting awkwardly and glancing off toward her dorm. But she was pleased with the idea of catching up with her older friend, so she said, "Well, what are you doing now? I just finished class and would die for a smoothie."

"I have one more class, but I'll be done in an hour. Meet me at the CowZone at say, 4:30?" Maya offered hopefully. "We'll catch up then?"

A wave of homesickness washed over Harper. Maybe Maya would have some advice on what classes to take next semester and also give her a taste of "the familiar" again.

"Sounds perfect! I'll just run back to my dorm and drop off my book bag. See you then!"

Maya and Harper sat in the bustling snack bar that used to be part of the old student cafeteria. They were mid-way through their smoothies, chatting about the freshman fifteen, roommates, and college boys.

"I've started dating someone — an older guy," Harper said with some hesitation, wondering what Maya would think about Jay.

"That's great, how did you two meet?" Maya asked.

Harper twisted the straw in her smoothie. "He's a junior teaching assistant in one of my classes. He's a philosophy and religion major."

"Really? So, is he a Christian?" Maya asked although she knew Blanchard didn't have a very "Christian" religion department.

"Uh, no I definitely wouldn't say he's a Christian. He's really more into self-discovery and inclusive religions. You know, like meditation. He's older, so he knows a lot more about these things." Harper said, feeling a need to defend him. "I've been learning so much about my inner self."

"Isn't that a bit New Age?" Maya asked. She remembered how popular meditation was when she first arrived at college. *I'm sure it's still a popular pastime for some students*, she thought, *since many students want to believe they still embrace spiritual things.*

"What made you want to try meditation?" she asked.

"I've taken a few classes and I think that Christianity and organized religion like that was maybe just a childhood phase. It doesn't seem to fit my life anymore."

Maya didn't speak for a moment, as she finished the last of her smoothie. Then she asked, "Are you sure? Some people might disagree with you on that. There are a lot more Christians here at Blanchard than you might think."

Harper pushed her hair behind her ears. "Well, I'm pretty happy right now. I've been learning so much from Jay. I want to be educated about truth and live my life in a way that makes sense to me and is not just based on stories from some ancient book."

"So, are you looking for truth, real truth about God?" Maya could see that Harper wasn't interested in a lecture about going to church or the Bible.

Harper looked down, playing with her straw. "Well, what

is the truth about God? Where is the evidence that God even exists? Evidence that creation isn't just some story Miss Roland told us in third grade? I don't think there's proof for any of it. Jay told me even his religion professor says Jesus was only a really good teacher." She went on, "I don't want to believe in childish stories anymore."

"I don't either," Maya replied.

Harper glanced up. "You don't? So, you agree with me?"

"Well, what if I told you that those weren't stories? What if there's reasonable evidence that God exists and that He created this world and everything in it for a purpose?

"For my first two years at Blanchard," Maya continued. "I was confused about God. I even questioned His existence, which made me start searching for the truth. You might be surprised at what I found. Would you like me to tell you about it?"

"What?" Harper was surprised. "You don't really think there's actual scientific evidence that God exists, do you? I mean, I'm taking biology and philosophy and I've read everything! Even my professors make it clear there's no reason to believe in God."

"Then you have nothing to worry about. In fact, let's look at whether there's reasonable evidence for all those things, and we won't even use the Bible. What do you think of that approach?"

Maya knew that evidence alone would not be enough. She knew everyone needed faith — even an atheist had to have faith to accept the theories that led to disbelief. But it was a good place to start.

Harper was suddenly excited that Maya was genuinely interested in discussing this further, and she was happy to reconnect with an old friend.

"Okay, well, I don't see how you'll be able to show evidence for all those things," Harper said. "But it would be interesting to see you try."

Maya was curious to know what kinds of questions Harper was struggling with. She ventured, "So when you think of the major challenges to Christianity, which ones come to mind?"

Harper thought for a moment, reflecting back on her classes and her time spent with Jay.

"Well there are five or six that come up pretty often," she said and quickly rattled them off —

- "There is no absolute truth
- There is no God
- If God were good, there would be no evil in the world
- Humans were produced through the evolutionary process of natural selection
- The Bible is just a book of stories and myths
- The Bible teaches Christians to hate non-Christians
- The Bible teaches Christians to hate others
- Jesus was a good teacher, but he wasn't God"

Maya was impressed at how quickly Harper could name some very important issues. It was clear Harper had developed strong reasoning behind her skepticism.

"That's quite a list. You and Jay must have had some deep discussions," Maya commented. Harper nodded.

"Let's make a deal," Maya continued. "We'll start meeting every week — every Tuesday at 4:30 — until all your challenges have been resolved. You just have to promise that you're going to come into this with an open mind, okay?"

An open mind? Harper thought to herself. "Dr. Meek says it's Christians who have closed minds, Maya," she protested.

"Well, I'll let you be the judge of that," Maya replied. "But how about we both commit to being open to the evidence? So what would you like to talk about first?"

Harper hesitated, "Jay says there's no absolute truth, that everyone determines truth for themselves. Let's start there."

Harper was sure the first week would show Maya how wrong she was and bring a quick end to their discussions.

But Maya was enthusiastic as they got up to leave the CowZone, "Next week — There is no absolute truth. See you then!"

"All right Maya, see you next Tuesday." Harper headed back to her dorm with confidence. *Maya will come to see that educated people don't believe in those old Bible myths,* she thought. Maybe she would invite Maya to start meditating with her and Jay.

Searching for More

1. Do you know of any evidence for God – outside of the Bible?

____

____

____

____

____

2. Have you ever questioned whether God really exists?

____

____

____

____

3. Did the characters of the Bible base their belief on faith or on evidence?

____

____

____

____

____

4. In what ways are science and religious beliefs the same?

____

____

____

____

5. Do you know any intelligent people who are Christians?

____

____

____

____

Sources for More Study

Books

- Dr. Norman Geisler, Ronald M. Brooks, *Come, Let Us Reason: An Introduction to Logical Thinking* (Baker Book House, 1990)

- S. Morris Engel, *With Good Reason* (New York, NY, St. Martin's Press, 1994)

- William L. Craig, *Hard Questions, Real Answers* (Wheaton, IL: Crossway Books, 2003)

Websites

- www.Impactapologetics.com
- www.Allaboutgod.com
- www.probe.org
- https://crossexamined.org/
- Reasonablefaith.org

Podcast

Breakpoint, the Colson Center for Christian Worldview
Host John Stonestreet talks about applying a Christian worldview to modern-day events

Videos/YouTube Channels

 https://youtu.be/lGWt43xCsZk?si=m_Q7mAbAdZIabWnl
Four Things I've Learned from Conversations with Atheists

 https://youtu.be/RY9ggdGGrjw?si=mfKoT9KNeQrxRFDh
Sean McDowell interviews Doug Groothuis, PhD Examining the Case for the Christian Faith

—2—

There is No Absolute Truth

"Everyone should be able to figure out truth for themselves!" Jay had insisted after Harper told him about her upcoming meeting with Maya. "Ask this friend of yours a simple question, 'Who gets to determine what truth is?' You can throw the Bible at me all you want, but that won't prove to me that truth comes from someone called God."

"She says she doesn't need the Bible to discuss truth," Harper cast a wondering look at Jay.

Jay chuckled. "Let's see how she does that — no Bible? That's going to take a miracle!" Jay laughed at his own joke.

Sometimes Jay ranted about God, the Bible, and religious types he called "easily gullible freaks" — people he encountered when he used to go to church. Despite his obvious disdain, Jay's points were clear and intelligent when he criticized people who quoted scripture and believed in God and Jesus.

When she first met Jay, Harper was a little offended at his open dislike for anyone who didn't share his anti-religious views. But, as she got to know him better, she was convinced his arguments were well thought-out and backed by pure philosophical examination. He'd already spent almost three years at Blanchard intensely researching philosophy, religion, and science for the honor's thesis he planned to write.

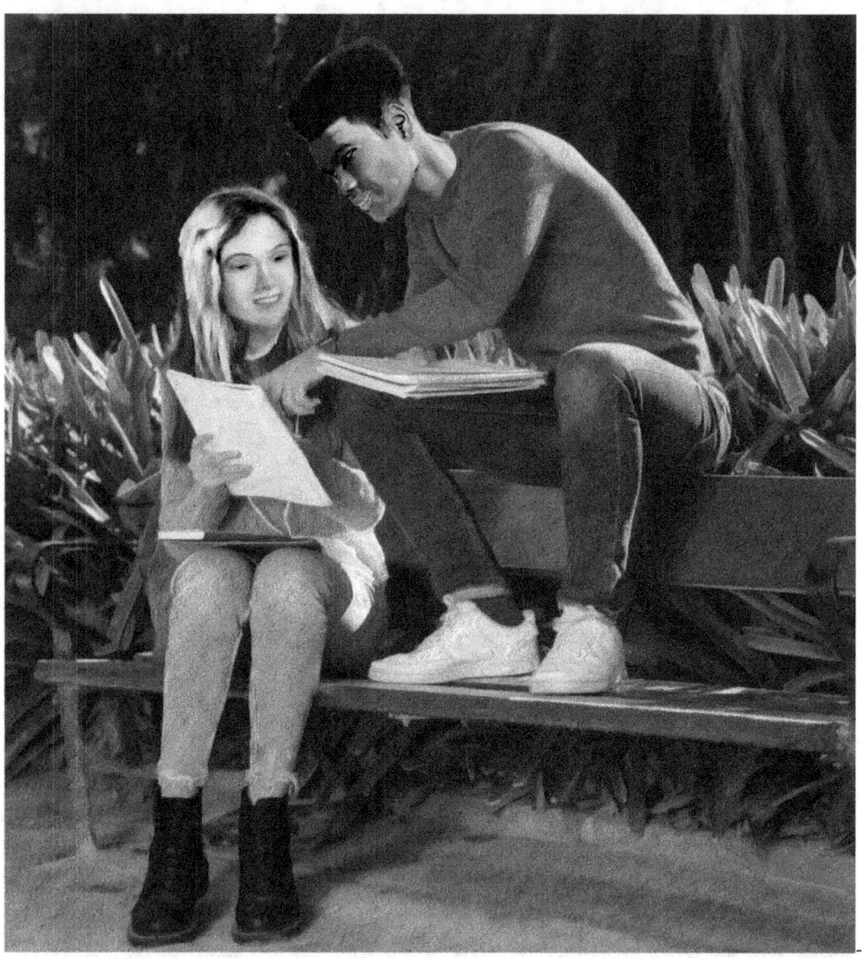

Harper wasn't sure she always understood Jay's reasoning, but the questions he brought up about who determines truth would prove that Maya was wrong. Like Jay always said,

"Religion is just a distraction facing the reality of life. It's the drug of choice for those who don't want to take responsibility. If they believe God is 'in control,' then they don't have to be accountable for what happens to them," he liked to say.

Although there was a twinge of bitterness in his tone when he talked like this, Harper saw his point and wondered if believing in God had always been just a way to avoid blame when things went wrong in her life.

When Maya texted her over the weekend to make sure they were still meeting on Tuesday, Harper decided to go ahead and test her with Jay's question. Knowing it would catch her off guard, she immediately texted, Who gets to decide what truth is anyway?

Maya was quick to text back, That's a great question, Harper. But if you want to talk about how to find truth, you should do a little research and come up with a clear definition of what you think truth is or what it should be, okay? Show me how you define truth.

Monday night, Harper was back in the library, attempting to find an answer to Maya's question. She took the assignment seriously, but the lack of concise information troubled her. The books and articles she examined claimed that all truth was relative. Religious and moral truth depended on the beliefs of the person.

Then is nothing objectively true? I just want to know that something is true, Harper thought. *How can truth be different for everyone?*

A few hours later, disappointed with the lack of definitive material, Harper gathered up her notes and left the library.

"Well, I couldn't figure out what truth is," she admitted to Maya the next day. "Almost every article I read said that all truth was relative to time, individuals, and situations. But that can't be right, can it? How can you make important decisions if you can't know what is true and what is false?"

"What do you think?" Maya asked, pleased that Harper had been considering this on her own. Maybe Harper wasn't completely influenced by everyone else's opinions.

"I mean, it seems there ought to be some things that are true all the time for everyone, but that's clearly not what most of the authors think. And Jay says that 'it's naïve to believe in the same truth for everyone all the time. Situations and people determine what is true.' But, I don't think I'm ignorant, and I believe truth should be something that's true no matter what anyone believes or feels. I just don't know where to find a definition of truth that makes sense to me."

"I recently read a book that, I think, describes your problem," Maya said. She took out a mint green notebook from her bag to read from a quote. "The author, Alisa Childers, explains truth like this:

> *"Truth is true for all people in all places and times. It's also something you can't invent, think up, or create. It is something you discover. It doesn't change, no matter how much people's beliefs about it do. Truth isn't altered because of how it makes someone feel."*[1]

"But, so many people say they know the truth, and they

all seem to describe it differently." Harper was struggling.

"Have you heard the story of the six blind men?" Maya asked, sensing Harper's confusion.

"No, what's it about?"

"Well, there's a fable told about six blind men who each examined an elephant. One man grabbed its tusk and said, 'Why this is a spear!'

"The next man grabbed its trunk and said, 'Oh my, a snake!' The third one put his arms around a leg and exclaimed, 'It's a tree!'

" 'I have a rope,' yelled the one who had its tail. Feeling the elephant's ear, the fifth man proclaimed, 'I've got a fan.'

"The last one ran into the elephant's side and shouted, 'This is a wall!' "

"Now can you tell me which one of these men is right?" Maya asked.

"None of them?" Harper responded, a bit perplexed.

"Sort of, but it's kind of a trick question. You're missing one. See, the one who is right is the one who's telling the story."[2]

"Oh, because he sees the whole animal and knows it's an elephant?" Harper asked, slowly beginning to understand. "While the others just experienced part of the elephant? So, why doesn't he just tell them they're only seeing part of the picture?" Harper thought the answer would be simple.

"Those articles you read are like the blind men proclaiming each has the truth. That's why truth seems to be relative to each person. Truth would be a very shallow reality then — if it were reality at all. Everyone would have a different story, and maybe all of them would miss the whole picture. Just like those blind men who didn't know what was right in front of them."

"So who sees the whole picture in our reality?"

Maya knew this was a very important starting point. "Like the elephant, truth is bigger than just you and me, Harper. Doesn't science teach us what is true is observable and repeatable? Scientists teach us to be skeptical of any evidence that is not discoverable; it's got to be bigger than the ideas of any individual."

"But what about Dr. Meek's view? He said truth cannot be absolute! And Jay agrees with him too. They say only Christians believe in Absolute Truth, and that a Christian's religious truth is only based on an out-of-date Bible." Harper resisted the argument.

Maya didn't hesitate with her answer, "Have you ever asked Jay how he is absolutely sure of that?"

"He says that *everyone* who is educated believes it, and anyone who doesn't believe it can't be very intelligent."

But Harper's voice didn't sound totally confident.

"So, according to Jay and Dr. Meek," Maya smiled at Harper and responded with a playful rhythm, "Absolutely everyone who is educated absolutely believes truth absolutely cannot be discovered? Is that right?"

Harper thought for a moment. She smiled, then started to laugh, "Okay, I think I'm getting your point. Dr. Meek and

Jay are being pretty absolute, aren't they?"

"Have you ever heard of the law of non-contradiction?" Maya was almost laughing too. When Harper shook her head, she continued, "Well, I think it was Aristotle who composed this logical argument, which says:

> *"One cannot say of something that it is, and that it is not, in the same respect and at the same time."*[2]

"So, what does that mean?" asked Harper.

"Well, for example, if the statement, 'The world is a sphere' is true, then at the same time, 'The world is flat' cannot also be a true statement. It must be one or the other. A statement cannot be both true and false at the same time and in the same respect; that's the law of non-contradiction."[3]

"So, when Dr. Meek claims that there absolutely cannot be an Absolute Truth, he is breaking the law of non-contradiction," Harper was catching on. "He's contradicting himself."

"So, the question is, how do we discover what is truth? Harper, how did you do it in science class?"

"We hypothesized, we carried out experiments, and we looked at the evidence," Harper responded.

"And that's the approach we should take here too. The evidence shows that there is universal truth; truth that has been true throughout history and across diverse societies. Now, we don't just look for the evidence, but we also get our hands dirty and test it. We can experiment, and when we eliminate what is false, the truth will remain. Despite what you may think, truth is all around us. Can you think of anything that is universally true in our society today?"

Harper took a deep breath, "Um, well, I would say it's universally wrong to steal. Is that what you mean?"

"Good example. You see, there really are truths in this world, and even an atheist believes that whether he admits it or not. Every society has adopted certain truths that transcend individuals; both good and bad things are judged similarly in almost every society. Laws are made that recognize these truths. There may be tyrants from time to time that try to overrule them, but eventually, society overcomes and reestablishes long-held common truths. There are some pretty obvious examples."

"Like murder, stealing, lying. I see what you mean." Harper sat for a moment, taking in the past hour of conversation. "I guess it is kind of silly to think that a person can determine truth."

"Well, it's certainly easier to think that we are only responsible to ourselves and we can all have our own version of the truth. That's called Relative Truth — beliefs that are based on opinion and preference or based on incomplete information. But we are searching for truth that never changes — Absolute Truth."

Maya saw Harper was beginning to understand the difference. "Well," Harper mused, "I want to know truth because I want to stand firm on something that is real. I want to believe in something that is there, no matter what I think about it. Truth that doesn't change because I change my mind or just because someone has a different perspective than I do."

Harper was now more anxious than ever. "But, how am I going to explain this to Jay?"

Maya knew Jay would want to hear about their discussion today. "I don't think you have to explain every detail to Jay just yet. But keep asking lots of questions without accepting arguments that merely *sound* intelligent. You may find that some people don't have as many answers as they want you to think. You know, some people believe it takes more faith to be an atheist than it does to be a Christian!"[4]

Maya went on, "Christian faith is not a matter of believing in something or someone who is unapproachable and unknowable. Quite the opposite is true. The God who made the universe also made it logical and orderly, and he reveals himself through the universe."

"But what if I don't believe that God exists anymore?" Harper knew this issue would be a very significant point with Jay and one she had personally wrestled with all semester.

"Then we have our question for next week – is there any evidence that God really exists? If, in fact, God exists, there should be evidence that he exists." Maya said enthusiastically.

Harper was relieved by her response and suddenly felt eager to meet again. "I can't wait to hear what you have to say about that! Jay says there is no evidence for the existence of God. And, he insists he won't believe in God until there is."

Harper was surprised to realize that Maya had not opened her Bible or even mentioned scripture for their entire discussion on truth. But she was certain Maya would resort to using Bible stories to discuss God.

"I guess I'll have to find my Bible?" Harper asked hesitantly. She could already imagine some of Jay's objections.

"There will be plenty to talk about without using that just

yet." Maya leaned down to grab a book from her bag and handed it to Harper. "In the meantime, here's a little something you might find interesting to read.

"But, I warn you, no amount of fact and logic will convince people who don't want to be convinced. That's why we talk about searching for both truth *and* faith. And that's why we're first going to search for truth, logically and scientifically, seeking evidence wherever possible. Where we find objective truth, it will have existed long before we came along, and it will remain long after we are gone. If God is who I believe he is, then there will be plenty of evidence for that outside of the Bible."

Searching for More

1. What beliefs do you have that you think are "universal?"

____

____

____

____

2. What problems would be solved if you alone could de-
    fine truth? What problems would be caused?

____

____

____

____

3. Is any one person capable of determining truth for every-
    one?

____

____

____

____

4. Can you name any truths that you base your life on?

____

____

____

____

____

5. How is your life more secure, or less secure, if you believe in Absolute Truths?

____

____

____

____

____

Sources for More Study

Books

- Dr. Norman Geisler, Ronald M. Brooks, *Come, Let Us Reason: An Introduction to Logical Thinking* (Baker Book House, 1990)

- S. Morris Engel, *With Good Reason* (New York, NY, St. Martin's Press, 1994)

- William L. Craig, *Hard Questions, Real Answers* (Wheaton, IL: Crossway Books, 2003)

Websites

- www.everystudent.com
- www.reasons.org

Podcasts

I Don't Have Enough Faith to be an Atheist, podcast hosted by Dr. Frank Turek, co-author of *I Don't Have Enough Faith to be an Atheist* and many other books on apologetics

Videos/YouTube Channels

William Lane Craig – Reasonable Faith
https://www.youtube.com/@ReasonableFaithOrg

Cold Case Christianity —Response to the statement: There are no objective moral truths
https://youtu.be/Dk166EukC_4?si=fK1eXeYEDlNctQTR

Daily Dose of Wisdom with Frank Turek — Atheist and Christian on Morality
https://youtu.be/2JXpzNPt67U?si=XlwYSGsH9AWkurt0

---

[1] Alisa Childers, *Live Your Truth and Other Lies* (Tyndale, 2022)

[2] Norman L. Geisler, Frank Turek, *I Don't Have Enough Faith To Be An Atheist* (Wheaton, ILL: Crossway Books, 2004) 48-49.

[3] Norman L. Geisler, Ronald M. Brooks, *Come Let Us Reason: An Introduction to Logical Thinking* (Grand Rapids, MI: Baker House Books, 1990) 16.

[4] Norman L. Geisler, Frank Turek, *I Don't Have Enough Faith To Be An Atheist* (Wheaton, ILL: Crossway Books, 2004)

—3—

There is No God

"It's a simple question with an impossible answer. How can you know?" Harper looked intently at Maya. They were back at the CowZone the following Tuesday, drinking smoothies at a table by the windows overlooking the quad.

"How can you know there's a God, you mean?" Maya asked.

"Yeah, outside of the Bible and Sunday school, of course. I know people say they have visions and see miracles and stuff, but I've never experienced any of that. I want real evidence that there is a real God." Harper seemed more intense than she had been last week.

Since her last meeting with Maya, Harper had briefly shared their discussion last week with Jay. She had found him unwavering in their discussion about absolute truth. She wasn't sure she wanted to argue with him about the existence of God — at least not without being very well prepared.

"Okay," Maya began, seeing Harper's genuine interest. "Well, let's start with some basic building blocks of science. What's the scientific explanation for the foundation of the universe?"

"Yeah...simple. Right!" Harper said sarcastically. Then she realized Maya was serious. "You mean we're going to actually talk about science?" She wasn't expecting this approach.

"Believe it or not, science is not the enemy of God that many people believe it is." Maya flipped to a page in the same green notebook she had pulled out the week before. "You might find this interesting — it's something Dr. Rebecca McLaughlin points out in her book, *Confronting Christianity* — it was two Franciscan friars who laid out the empirical and methodological foundations for the scientific method.[1] Most universities, like Harvard and Yale, were founded by Christian churches to explore both truth and science. Christians believed then, and also now, that the two should support each other.

"Today there are scientists who are unwilling to consider any explanations that may include the existence of God, but the discipline of science is a great tool for discovering truth. I mean, science teaches us how to prove things, right?"

"Yeah, I guess, but what does this have to do with finding evidence for God?" Harper was perplexed.

"Sorry, I'm getting to that. So, back to scientific basics, do you remember Mr. Grady's AP physics class?"

"Of course! He was one of my favorite teachers. He always explained everything so well," Harper said with enthusiasm, despite her uncertainty that physics would be able to prove God's existence.

"Well, what do you remember about the First Law of Thermodynamics?" Maya asked.

Harper had to think about it for a minute. "Um, if I remember correctly, the First Law says that matter and energy in the universe are finite. No new energy is being added."

"Exactly! How in the world did you remember that?" Maya had underestimated Harper's memory of high school physics and Mr. Grady's teaching techniques.

"In other words, our universe had to have a beginning! Maybe you remember the Second Law of Thermodynamics, too?"

"The Second Law says that everything is falling apart. What was the word he used? 'Entropy.' The first law is ENERGY, and the second law is ENTROPY. Mr. Grady liked to make up little tunes to help us study for his tests. Do you remember the song he taught us?"

Maya laughed, "Yeah, I remember people humming the tune during the final, but to get back on topic, you're right again. So, the first Law says the universe had to have a beginning and the second says that it has to come to an end. In the book I gave you last week, you may have read that Geisler and Turek believe the universe is sort of like a clock that has been wound up and is slowly running down.[2]

"While the amount of time it's been running and how long it will run is under debate, no scientist I know of disputes these laws: the universe had a beginning and will have an end. So, here's the Billion Dollar Question, 'Who wound it up in the first place?' "

"You mean, how did it all start? I would say it just happened spontaneously with the Big Bang. Isn't that what all scientists believe?" Harper asked.

"Today, most scientists believe in the Big Bang, but not long ago almost every scientist believed the Big Bang was just another concoction manufactured by creationists. However, when more powerful telescopes were invented and satellites were put into space, then more accurate cosmic measurements could be made of the expanding universe. There is clear evidence today that the massive universe that we have now began from a point smaller than the head of a pencil…another fact that scientists initially labeled as just another religious myth."

Harper assumed scientists had always believed in the Big Bang theory. She sat there quietly listening and wondering how scientists could be so dogmatic about the "facts" and then change their "proven" theories as soon as more data was available.

Maya waited a minute and then moved on, "Now, we also know the universe is a complex place; the earth itself is just an incredibly small part of the overall universe. Scientists are still improving the accuracy of their measurement techniques, but it certainly appears to be billions of light years across."

Harper couldn't hold back, "So you think the universe is billions of years old? I thought most Christians thought it was only thousands of years old." Jay thought Christians were stupid for rejecting carbon dating and other methods that "proved" the earth was more than a billion years old.

"Well, for now, the point isn't so much the age of the universe as the fact that scientific research confirms that it had a beginning. And, even more important for our discussion, research continues to confirm the vast complexity of the universe. Millions of planets, billions of light years across, all connected in gravity and space, in a universe that's continuously expanding and continuously using up a finite amount of energy.

"Once scientists proved the expansion of the universe, it was only simple math to determine that it had to start somewhere at some point in time. And, if it started somewhere, at some point in time, then something had to have caused it to begin — *Something* could not have come from *Nothing*!

"Have you ever noticed just how much stuff is up there? How did it get there?" Maya took a breath and pointed upward.

"Yeah, I went camping in the mountains and just seeing the clear night sky, you know, away from the city? It seems like you can see millions of stars. And what we can see is just a tiny part of it! I've heard the Webb telescope has now discovered there are billions of stars more than scientists had previously thought existed!" Harper said, excited about the wonders of the universe she'd seen on her trip.

She was beginning to put the pieces together, "So, the evidence shows that *Something* started from *Nothing*. And, then it had to be wound up and turned loose. And now, what was once *Nothing* is billions of years across and very complex. And all this points to an intelligent source for creation. Is that it?"

"Bingo! And now scientists know that the universe is finely tuned — just like a finely tuned instrument precisely adjusted to create perfect notes. Without fine-tuning, the best instruments are worthless.

"If things like gravity, the speed of light, and the amount of energy in the universe were any different, even minutely different, not only would Earth not support human life, but the entire universe would have collapsed soon after creation.[3]

"But, let me also tell you about something much smaller, and yet just as complex. You remember that Darwin thought everything started with just one cell, right?" Maya continued without looking up. Flipping to a blank page in her notebook, she turned Harper's focus to another scientific subject.

"What do you know about E. coli?" Maya began to draw a picture of a cell. At first, it was a simple circle, but she began to detail the different parts as described in her textbook.

"Um, people get pretty sick from eating it," Harper was having trouble following Maya's logic. "Wait, what does E. coli have to do with anything?"

Maya laughed. "I studied E. coli in my biology class just last week. It turns out E. coli is a very complex cell. It has what's called a bacterial flagellum, a tiny engine that enables the bacteria to move. That little motor is made of 40 different proteins, but you can only see them by magnifying it fifty thousand times!"

"Wow." Harper was amazed. "Talk about the little engine that could!"

"Yeah, and that tiny little motor runs at 100,000 rpm! But, it can also stop on a dime, shift directions, and start spinning 100,000 rpm in the opposite direction. It has two gears, forward and reverse, and is water-cooled and hardwired to read data from its surrounding environment."[4]

"Interesting," Harper was suddenly distracted by a group of loud sorority girls who had just burst into the CowZone. Harper had decided back in August that rushing a sorority didn't align with her pursuit of law school and being taken seriously as an intellectual. *They all probably believe in religion, anyway,* she thought. She was certain Jay would agree with her.

"Hey, what kind of car do you drive?" Maya decided to

change the subject again.

Harper turned back, her face lit up, "Last year, my parents bought me one of those new hybrids for graduation! I honestly never thought they would, but it is a really cool car!"

"Wow, I've heard those hybrids are awesome! I'm not sure exactly how it works with both electric and gas," Maya confessed. She was excited, too, because she thought it might make a perfect example of complexity for Harper.

Immediately, Harper launched into an enthusiastic description of her new car. She explained how the electric engine runs at low speeds, saving the gas engine for when more power is needed. "It automatically knows when to cut the gas engine on and off! With the way the car is designed, there's no need to recharge the batteries either. They recharge on their own through a generator tied to both the engine and the braking system. I never have to recharge the batteries. It does it automatically. It's kind of an engineering miracle!" Harper beamed.

"So, I guess some genius has been working on creating it for a few years, huh?"

"Well, Maya, it wasn't by accident," Harper sounded a little condescending. "Teams of geniuses had to spend a lot of time thinking about building something that complicated!"

Harper was proud of her car; not only was she doing her part for the environment, but this car was also an engineering work of art. *I'd love to meet the incredible brain behind it!* Harper thought. She imagined a bespectacled engineer sitting in a white coat surrounded by computers and lots of other intelligent-looking people with long lists of credentials behind their names.

Maya drew her imagination back to science, "Well, how about the E. coli? The bacterial flagellum is incredibly complex, too. I called it a motor not just because it propels the bacteria, but because motors are seemingly the product of intelligent design, right? The E. coli bacteria may be tiny, but in many ways, its systems are just as complicated as your hybrid. If you remove any one part, the entire system will fail. What if I told you the engineering of your new car was the product of some random chance?"

"I'd say you were completely insane," Harper jumped in, thinking again about her vision of the engineer.

Maya laughed, "There's a lot of intelligence involved in the complex organization of E. coli, or literally billions of other products of creation. Billions of stars, millions of galaxies, intricately connected and operating in a perfect solar system — so large that even our untamed imaginations fall far short; delicate flowers and armies of insects that depend upon one another and impact other plants, larger animals, and even entire ecosystems. There are thousands of observations scientists can make today that Darwin could not make. Virtually every day, discoveries are made that bring scientists closer and closer to understanding the intricacies of our vast and complex universe."

Harper sat back in her chair. "I never even thought about science like that..." now she was almost whispering, "as giving evidence of God's existence."

"Here, read what Geisler and Turek say in their book," Maya said as she handed her earmarked copy to Harper.

> *" 'If there is no God, why is there something rather than nothing?' Is a question that we all have to answer. And in light of the evidence, we are left with only two options: either no one created something out of nothing, or else someone created something out of nothing. Which view is more reasonable?"* [5]

Harper put the book down and stared at the bottom of her smoothie cup, playing with her straw. "Ever since I came to college, people made me think that God was just a myth and that no logical argument would prove his existence."

Maya offered her understanding. "Never forget that while many people would try to convince you to believe that, no one can *make* you believe anything. You always have the option of digging for truth yourself. And, truthfully, the Christian church hasn't always done a good job of educating its believers, either. Faith is absolutely important, but we also have the evidence to back it up."

With kindness in her voice, she continued. "Harper, no amount of proof will make someone believe in God, even when it's logical to do so. I believe there is powerful evidence that it's the best explanation for the world that we live in, but others may think differently and may never change their minds."

Maya wasn't quite finished. "Even Albert Einstein, in the face of scientific evidence, changed from believing there is no God to believing in some kind of intelligent creator. The evidence was too strong for one of the smartest scientists in history to remain an atheist.[6]

"But, there is non-scientific evidence as well," Maya continued. "For instance, is there a logical reason why every society agrees with basic moral laws? As we talked about last week, every society that we have been able to study throughout history agrees that things like lying, stealing, and murder, for instance, are wrong. Why is there such consistency in moral laws unless there is a primary source for morality?

"The most logical deduction is there must be an intelligent law-giver that has influenced every society on earth. Can you think of a logical reason why, as humans, we are natural seekers? We are curious by nature, and as a species, we alone long to find the answers to everything. It's reasonable to suggest that the longing for the ultimate search was implanted in us — finding out where we all came from and who brought us into being.

"Again, it may involve faith, but there is a logical, reasonable rationale behind the conclusion. Every other solution requires even more faith, and sometimes even very illogical reasoning.

"Let me find this quote from Lee Strobel in his book, *The Case for Faith*." Maya took the book out and flipped until she found the page she was looking for.

> *" …without God, there is no absolute right and wrong that imposes itself on our conscience. But we know deep down that objective moral values do exist – some actions like rape and child torture, for example, are universal moral abominations — and, therefore, this means God exists."* [7]

"This is going to require some thinking," Harper's mind was full. Too full. She needed a nice long jog to give her time to process. It was almost more information than she could handle at one time, especially about such an important subject. She was beginning to feel the same way she had during those first few weeks with Dr. Meek.

She knew Jay would be anxious to hear how Maya had "brainwashed" her this week, and she wanted to prepare for a discussion with him. Her perspectives were changing, and she needed a moment to decide what to say.

Maya interrupted her thoughts, "So, is there a topic you had in mind for next week?" She began to pack up the notes and the books she had brought.

Harper was also thinking about their next discussion but wasn't quite ready to give Maya an answer.

"Can I text you?" Harper was sure she had other questions she wanted answered, too. They stood up at the same time and threw their cups in the trash.

"Yeah, just let me know. Same time next week?" Maya wasn't sure what Harper had in mind, or if perhaps her commitment was waning.

"Yes, same time. I'll be back, don't worry. You haven't scared me off yet," Harper said, reading the inquisitive look on Maya's face. She pushed open the swinging doors into the fading sunshine. It was the perfect weather for an early evening jog.

Searching for More Evidence

1. What evidence, if it existed, would convince you to believe Christianity is true? If you found it to be true, would you commit your life to being a Christian?

____

____

____

____

____

2. The Bible says there has been evidence for God from the beginning of the world. What is an example of this evidence?

____

____

____

____

____

3. What evidence do you believe exists to support the
    position that there is no God?

____

____

____

____

4. What evidence for the absence of God do you feel is the
    weakest?

____

____

____

____

____

5. What are some additional moral arguments for the
    existence of God?

____

____

____

____

Sources for More Study

Books

- Dr. Norman Geisler, Frank Turek; *I Don't Have Enough Faith to Be an Atheist* (Wheaton, Illinois: Crossway Books, 2004)

- Ravi Zacharias, Norman Geisler, *Who Made God?* (Grand Rapids, MI: Zondervan, 2003)

- C.S. Lewis, *Mere Christianity* (New York, NY, HarperCollins Publishers, reprint 1980)

- William Dembski, *Intelligent Design* (Intervarsity Press, 1999)

Websites

- www.Allaboutscience.org
- www.Allaboutphilosophy.org
- www.gocampus.org
- www.discover.com
- Christianity.com

Podcast

Reasonable Faith — Podcast host William Lane Craig is a leading Christian philosopher.

Videos/YouTube Channels

**Frank Turek Channel – Cross-Examined
The Uncaused First Cause**
https://youtu.be/ApVEMbyeL14?si=_HWu-CGq8EIKY9pW2

**Frank Turek: I Don't Have Enough Faith to be
an Atheist**
https://youtu.be/en8dJyc9Vto?si=ZKcjlD9wRz4rtNpl

---

[1] Norman L. Geisler, Frank Turek, *I Don't Have Enough Faith to Be an Atheist* (Wheaton, ILL: Crossway Books, 2004)

[2] Michael J. Behe, *Darwin's Black Box*, (New York, NY: Touchstone, 1996) 69-72

[3] William Dembski, *Intelligent Design*, (Intervarsity Press, 1999)

[4] Michael J. Behe, *Darwin's Black Box*, (New York, NY: Touchstone, 1996) 69-72

[5] Norman L. Geisler, Frank Turek, *I Don't Have Enough Faith to Be an Atheist* (Wheaton, ILL: Crossway Books, 2004)

[6] ibid.

[7] Lee Strobel, *The Case for Faith* (Grand Rapids, MI: Zondervan, 2000) 348

—4—

If God is Good, Why is There Evil in the World?

Harper walked into the CowZone on Tuesday a little early. She and Jay had been on campus talking about her conversations with Maya.

They'd been discussing those meetings a lot lately, and Jay was visibly frustrated with Harper's newly acquired challenges to his anti-Christian arguments. She'd continued to process what Maya had talked about, and from time to time, she wrote questions in the margins of her notes during class. She was growing more and more confident in her skepticism of the anti-Christian mindset and often relayed this to Jay.

But he was secretly gaining respect for Maya's logical approach to the questions and for Harper's calm way of pushing back on his ideas.

He'd only heard Christians argue "with a Bible in one hand and a hammer in the other," as he phrased it. But Maya's approach seemed to be refreshingly different.

However, one thing had been bothering him lately — if God was love and goodness and all that, why was there evil in the world?

"There's just no way I could believe in a good God — if he ever did exist," Jay stated matter-of-factly at dinner the previous Saturday night.

Harper explained to Jay why she believed there was

provable and solid scientific evidence of God's existence.

"You may think that he 'wound everything up,' but maybe he's not around anymore. Or maybe he's up there somewhere and just doesn't care about us. How could a good God tolerate all the evil and suffering we see in the world?"

Jay was obviously stuck on this dilemma and Harper knew her immediate answers would be too shallow. Pushing the food around on her plate, Harper nervously invited him to come to the next discussion. To her surprise, Jay agreed to go, as long as it didn't interfere with his school schedule. She decided to text Maya later that evening and tell her she'd found the topic for the meeting and might be bringing a guest.

At the CowZone on Tuesday, Harper sat down to wait for Maya, anxious to have answers for Jay and herself about the puzzling reason for suffering. The weather was colder now, so she had ordered a latte instead of a smoothie or milkshake.

She sat at their regular table by the window, looking out at the swarm of students hurrying across the brick sidewalk through the quad to their next class. Her mind drifted to thinking about the many homeless and hungry people in the world. *God is supposed to be good*, she thought. She'd seen poverty firsthand in her own little town growing up and got lost in thought. She didn't see Maya walk in.

"A little early today, Harper?" Maya was impressed. Harper had been right that she wasn't scared off, and Maya had been proud of the sincerity she had shown over the past few weeks.

Harper snapped back to the present moment, "Oh, hi...yeah, Jay and I were hanging out earlier, but he had to work on a project with a group from his class. So, I just came in to wait," she said. "He might drop in later if that's okay." She hoped it would be sooner rather than later. She found Maya's explanations to be clearer first-hand.

"Definitely! I'd love the chance to finally meet him!" Maya said with a smile. Maya was excited but wondered how open Jay would be. "I hope you haven't been waiting too long, but I have a feeling today is going to be worth the wait; this is a topic I struggled with for a long time." She took off her jacket and sat down.

"Really?" Harper laughed nervously. "So, Jay and I aren't the only ones?"

Maya laughed too, "No, you are most certainly not the only ones. In fact, this question gets asked a great deal."

"Well, I tried looking in the Bible, but I didn't see anything that directly answers the question. Besides, Jay isn't really into the Bible anyway. I'm not sure he would have believed anything I said that was based solely on the Bible."

"Well, let's look at the question without the Bible for now. The Bible isn't the only source for understanding why bad things happen."

"Then we are definitely in for an interesting discussion today!" The deep voice came from Jay, who had walked up behind Harper with an armful of muffins and napkins. "Our study group got moved to Thursday and they were handing out free refreshments in the quad, so I grabbed some and headed here." He handed them out to the girls.

"Hi — Jay Trotman," he said, holding out his free hand to shake Maya's.

"I'm Maya. So glad you could come!" Maya responded, pleased that Jay had made it.

"Yeah, thanks for getting us these." Harper peeled the wrapper off her muffin and took a quick bite, a little nervous about how Jay would interact with Maya.

"Yes, thank you! And you haven't missed a thing!" Maya said, already thinking she could see why Harper had been attracted to his friendly face and confident stride.

"You're welcome," he said, taking the chair next to Harper. "All right, Maya, tell me, if God created everything, didn't he create evil, too?"

Maya could see Jay wasn't going to waste any time getting to the topic, "Well, if you think of creation as an intentional act, then no, I don't believe that God created evil. God is 100% good and that means he is 100% evil-free."

Jay had thought about the question many times and was prepared to question her thoroughly. "So, are you denying the existence of evil? Harper told me that you believe there are absolute truths of good and evil. But it sounds like you don't really believe that after all."

"Quite the opposite, Jay. There is no question in my mind that bad things happen all the time. In fact, bad things happen to good people all the time." Maya was anticipating his next question.

Harper joined the dialogue with her own concerns, "Couldn't God have made us so we could only do good things? Wouldn't a good God," she hesitated, now looking at Jay and knowing what he was thinking, "wouldn't a good God create a world without evil?"

Harper was genuinely perplexed. *God could make us stop doing bad things,* she thought. *He could make us just be good.*

"Well, let me ask you both a question, then. What does it mean to love someone unconditionally?" Maya asked.

Jay and Harper looked at each other. Jay responded. "It seems love is a different subject, but I'll play along." He thought for a moment, and then responded, "I guess it means no matter what a person does, you still love them."

"So, if I love someone who never does anything wrong, is that unconditional love?" Maya asked.

"Well, it would at least be untested love." Jay was beginning to follow her logic.

"How could God demonstrate his ultimate love for mankind, if, in fact, people were always lovable, if there were no evil?" Maya had struggled a long time with this question herself.

"I guess that's a good point. So, are you saying God created evil so that he could prove that he was a loving God?"

Jay wasn't quite ready to accept Maya's position.

"Think about it another way. If God created people who were only capable of loving him in return, then how would that demonstrate love and goodness? Wouldn't that be the act of a selfish God, one who only allowed people to do what he wanted them to do? Would you believe someone is good who orchestrated every single decision you make?"

Harper shuddered, "We would have no freedom in any aspect of our lives. We would be little zombies. We might not be killing each other or suffering any physical pain but we certainly would not love one another or love God either…at least not genuinely. And I'm not sure you could say God is a loving God if he only loves people who are always doing peaceful and kind things — things he forced them to do…"

But Jay still pressed the point, "What about all the bad things that just happen? Nobody gives another person cancer. Maybe your good God causes that. Why would God give someone cancer?"

"I know I don't have all of the answers. But on this issue, I think there's a somewhat simple way to look at it."

Maya grabbed a napkin and drew a squiggly line. Pointing to it, she asked, "What is that?"

"I'm not much of an artist, and it's obvious you aren't either. But, that's a crooked line," Harper spoke up, pretending to frown at the line Maya had drawn.

"How do you know?" Maya looked up from the paper. "What if I said it was a straight line?"

Jay took the pencil from her and drew a long line across the napkin. "That's a straight line, see the difference?" He had used the same logic in his first philosophy class. He had never thought to apply the simple concept to the problem of good and evil. "You're saying that bad things happen just so we can appreciate good things?"

"Well, I admit that only God knows the reason behind tragedy. But what you often see in those situations can present a paradox — People doing good things in bad situations — pretty amazing." Maya spoke more softly now; she and her family had experienced tragedy in the past. She knew that simple answers were not enough.

Harper was suddenly reminded of Maya's brother, Rishi. He'd been in a terrible car accident driving home from college for summer break. He was left unconscious and eventually died from severe injuries.

Maya turned and explained to Jay what had happened two years ago. "My brother was in a coma for weeks, and we were stunned at the way people responded to us. We didn't go to the grocery store or cook meals for months. More than thirty people gave blood to replenish the transfusions that he had to have.

"Over five hundred people came to his funeral, and the cards and letters we received were overwhelming. I'm not saying that any of that replaced the pain and sorrow we felt, but we saw goodness and compassion in people that we had never seen before. How could we have observed those characteristics in people we didn't even know without this tragedy?"

Neither Harper nor Jay knew what to say. But they were clearly touched by her experience.

"Our family came to know God more deeply, to depend on him in ways that we had never experienced before. But we also came to know other people in ways that left a strong and lasting impression of their character and love for us. I'm not saying that God caused my brother's accident; I can't claim to understand the entirety of God's plan. But I am sure that he used it for good in the lives of many people.

"I think a really good God can take even terrible things and use them for good." Maya had spent many tearful nights searching to understand the goodness of God since the loss of her only brother.

"We had to consider how God dealt with suffering and death too," Maya continued. "What we know and believe about God is that even he does not avoid suffering. At least we know from the story of Jesus — told both by the Bible and many sources outside of the Bible — that Jesus suffered greatly. Rebecca McLaughlin points out that Jesus himself was subjected to a great deal of suffering. She reminds us that, at the very least, atheists lead us to believe there is no purpose in suffering, whereas Jesus tells us there is reason and purpose, and he promises a future without suffering.[1] We learned a great deal about what suffering is and how God can bring good out of evil."

"I am so sorry about Rishi. It must have been so hard to come back to school without him there." Harper looked away, thinking about the emptiness she would feel if her little brother were to die so suddenly.

"It's still pretty hard at times, but we often see God's goodness at work. And I'm the best evidence of that goodness, especially in suffering and heartache. One of my favorite authors is C.S. Lewis. He was a Christian philosopher who suffered tragedy, too. He once wrote that,

> *"God whispers to us in our pleasures, speaks in our con-science, but shouts in our pain. It's his megaphone to rouse a deaf world.* [2]

"God has a reason for all things, especially suffering, even if we never know what that reason is. C.S. Lewis later wrote another book, *A Grief Observed*, after he suffered the loss of his wife to cancer. He struggled, but still saw God's powerful presence amid his pain."

As they continued to talk back and forth, Jay was moved

by both Maya's personal experience and her answers to his questions. He had not expected to hear any logical reasons for evil in the world. But he was ready to ask another question.

"I'm sorry, too, about your brother. And I understand how you can see good come from it. But I'm not ready to admit that your good God brought everything into existence. Doesn't it bother you that God started all this stuff with a Big Bang and left everything else to chance?"

"I don't believe things happen randomly, Jay. But it sounds like you're on another topic now! Are you asking me if I believe random chance brought about the creation of humans?" Maya wasn't about to concede this point.

Jay tried not to roll his eyes. "You don't believe that God specifically created Adam and Eve, do you? That's just more mythology!"

Maya wasn't going to argue this point just yet, "I have to get to the library to finish a psych paper, but it seems to me that you both need to come back next week, and we'll talk about evolution. You tell me your views on evolution and I'll explain the scientific basis for the Bible's view of creation."

"Done." His love for debate was one of the reasons Jay pursued philosophy as a major. And he enjoyed arguing that man was just a result of random chance. *This is going to be fun*, he thought.

But he knew he was going to have to rethink some of his objections to the existence of God.

Searching for More

1. What is the worst thing that ever happened to you? Who caused it?

____

____

____

____

2. Have you ever felt that something that happened to you was unfair? Did it make you doubt the existence of a good God?

____

____

____

____

3. If God treated you fairly, what would be different about your life today?

____

____

____

____

4. G.K. Chesterton said, "Without God, there would be no atheists." What do you think he means by that?

____

____

____

____

____

5. What lessons have you learned from suffering?

____

____

____

____

____

Sources for More Study

Books

- Lee Strobel, *The Case for Faith*, (Grand Rapids, MI: Zondervan, 2000)

- C.S. Lewis, *The Problem of Pain* (New York, NY: HarperCollins Publishers, reprint 1996)

- C.S. Lewis, *A Grief Observed* (New York, NY: HarperCollins Publishers, reprint 1996)

- Rebecca McLaughlin, *Confronting Christianity* (Wheaton, IL, Crossway, 2019)

Websites

- www.bethinking.org
- www.ses.edu
- www.equip.org
- www.josh.org

Podcast

Think Biblically, hosted by Scott Rae and Sean McDowell, professors at Biola University's Talbot School of Theology

Videos/YouTube Channels

 **Geisler Channel – Norm Geisler International Ministry**
https://youtu.be/LjUlHU5oDeE?si=odTYzf9s03rHpKv3
If God, Why Evil?

 **Frank Turek— visit to Compass Bible Church**
https://youtu.be/V2eNyrknOAk?si=x7RNfjc9x1t3zrOv
If God, Why Evil?

---

[1] Rebecca McLaughlin, *Confronting Christianity* (Wheaton, IL, Crossway, 2019) 206

[2] C.S. Lewis, *The Problem of Pain* (New York, NY: HarperCollins Publishers, reprint 1996) 93

—5—

Science Proves That Man is a Product of Evolution and Natural Selection

The following week was unusually warm, so the women chose a table outside in the sun for their chat. They caught up briefly on news from home until Jay joined them soon after.

"Well, what did you two find out about evolution?" asked Maya.

Harper pulled out her notes. It had been a long week of research, especially with all the schoolwork she had to finish. She'd hardly seen Jay at all. He, too, had been busy with other commitments; besides, he was already familiar with *The Origin of Species* and *The Descent of Man*, Darwin's books outlining his theory of evolution.

But Harper had been somewhat surprised to hunt beneath the surface only to find evolutionary "facts" that often turned out to contradict one another or were really just theories and unproven ideas. She'd expected to find scientifically proven explanations. She also couldn't find any articles in the library that supported any theories other than Darwinism. It seemed any idea was considered possible unless it included the possibility of God.

So Harper summarized the popular theory, "Well, evolution claims that life — the entire world we live in — came from single cells that were the result of the random matching of amino acids and proteins."

"You mean man came from a random action of primitive chemicals, with no purpose or direction?" Maya asked.

"Yeah, we all came from a single cell." Harper felt she was as prepared as possible, considering the absence of competing evidence in the college library. She and Jay had discussed it after their philosophy class. Although she still had reservations, Jay had already concluded that evolution was a scientific "slam dunk."

Jay found the previous week's discussion on good and evil different than he expected. He'd actually enjoyed it. No one had ever challenged his anti-religious views so effectively. He found it surprising that someone who had faith in God also had answers to his questions on evil and suffering. At first, he was irritated, but this past week, something seemed to change in his attitude. Harper wondered if Maya's arguments were beginning to get through to him. They were definitely changing Harper's mind. She'd even joined Maya at church this past week. The large number of college students there and the more casual setting had been very different from the formal church she attended at home.

Still, there's no reason to go off the deep end, she thought. *Evolution is still the only scientific answer for the creation of man. And what difference does it make? Even the preacher at my old church said God could have used evolution to produce man.*

Maya was anxious to hear more about Harper's evidence for evolution. "Okay, so teach me about it. Pretend I'm a monkey and don't know anything about evolution. Tell me how I get to be a human."

Harper laughed and looked across the table at Jay. He had coached her on how to explain the theory and planned to let her do most of the talking.

"Darwin believed that life began with a single cell," she began, "then through a process of progressive mutations, simple cells eventually formed into plants and animals. This process of mutation, using what he called 'natural selection,' produced stronger, more complex forms of life. Eventually, over billions of years, this evolutionary process brought human beings into existence."[1]

She glanced at Jay and he winked his approval. "So," she continued, "he wanted to prove why different organisms have similar structures like arms, legs, fins, wings, mouths, gills, and eyes, but don't all have the same complexity or use them in the same way," Harper added. "According to Darwin, that all started from one cell."

"So where did that first cell come from?" Maya wanted to explore the theory a little further.

Harper was less sure of the answer to that question. Skimming her notes, she replied, "Well, Darwin didn't really talk about that. He didn't concentrate on uncovering the creation of the first cell, just the development of it. It was a Roman Catholic priest, Lemaître, who published the original idea of the Big Bang, based on the theory of general relativity and the cosmological principle. And you were right — most scientists didn't generally believe in the Big Bang until the 1960s." Harper looked up to see Maya raising her eyebrows.

"You're forgetting that I'm supposed to be a monkey here. Monkeys don't know what a Big Bang is."

"Oh, right, I forgot. According to my old textbooks, scientists believe a hyperexplosion, or at least a huge expansion, occurred almost 14 billion years ago and the universe has been expanding ever since. Most cosmologists and physicists today accept that the Big Bang is the best model for the universe's origin."

"So the Big Bang is where the first living cell came from?" Maya challenged Harper to think deeper.

Harper flipped through her notebook, "Well remember the first cell came from the combination of amino acids and proteins," Harper reminded her. "Ah, here are my notes on this: two scientists, Miller and Urey, came up with this experiment where they put water, methane, ammonia, and hydrogen together to recreate the chemical conditions of the earth right after the Big Bang and actually produced amino acids, which are used to make proteins in living cells. They proved that the origin of life occurred through chemical evolution."

"Really? But, I have another question. What if some of the best scientists in the world believed that primitive Earth never had any methane or ammonia?" Maya had read up on Miller and Urey's experiment and knew more than Harper realized.

"Um, well," Harper struggled to find an answer, trying to remember if she had read anything about that. "I don't really know." Jay shifted in his seat, as he looked up at the sky and tried to avoid Harper's glance. He seemed to be perplexed as well.

"In the 1980s, NASA scientists discovered that primitive Earth didn't have enough of either methane or ammonia or hydrogen to amount to anything and instead was composed of water and CO_2 and nitrogen—not amino acids and proteins. In fact, no modern experiments have been able to demonstrate a viable explanation for the origin of the first cell."[2]

"I thought you were supposed to be a monkey, not a scientist!" Jay finally interjected.

Maya laughed. "Well, let's pretend I'm now a very smart monkey."

Jay was determined to continue the debate, "Look, every biology professor I've ever known believes that if chemicals had an ample amount of time to interact in the warm little ponds of primitive Earth — and I would say that 14 billion years is a lot of time — eventually life would emerge."

"Jay, time is not just the answer, it's part of the problem. Is fourteen billion years long enough? Is that enough time to produce something very complex from absolutely nothing? You would think that science, of all disciplines, would say that no amount of time is enough to produce something out of nothing."

Maya let Harper and Jay think about this fact for a minute. Then she continued. "Remember just how complicated even the tiniest living cells are; imagine them mutating over eons from one form to the next on their path to becoming humans.

"A world-renowned British astronomer and mathematician from Cambridge University determined that creating a unique earth that would support life and then evolve life into the highly complex organisms called humans would even take far longer than fourteen billion years. He stated that it would be similar to a tornado tearing through a junkyard and randomly assembling a fully functional Boeing 747 airplane.[12] What is the possibility of that? How many tornadoes would that take over how many billions of years? You see the problem?"[3]

Sounds impossible, Harper thought to herself, *but it seems that most scientists still believe it could happen.* Yes, she was starting to see the problem with the theory of random evolution. *Maybe it really is no more than a theory, and not even a very defensible one at that. How can something come from nothing?*

"Well, I brought along another book to help us out with this topic; I think it explains it better than I can." Maya pulled out a copy of Michael Behe's *Darwin's Black Box.* "Behe is a well-respected biochemist. And in this book, Behe talks about chemical evolution and the probability of those amino acids creating life as we know it. He calls his theory 'irreducible complexity.' He uses some other analogies, too. He said that the likelihood of linking together just one hundred amino acids to produce one protein molecule by chance would be the same as a blindfolded man finding one marked grain of sand somewhere in the middle of the Sahara Desert. And not just doing it one time, but three times."[4]

"Okay, but that still doesn't prove that God did it," Jay challenged. He was determined to make a case for evolutionary mutation. "Darwin spent a lot of time doing scientific experiments to form his theories, and they have been almost universally accepted by the scientific community."

Maya folded her arms over the book, leaning on the table. "In a broad sense, they have. But remember, Darwin was a scientist in the 1800s, long before modern techniques and equipment were available. New discoveries are constantly eroding the theories of evolution, which is why Michael Behe examines Darwin's theories in an attempt to understand them more fully. In the end, though, Behe unveils something that Darwin himself stated. Even Darwin recognized the limits of science. In summarizing his own works, Darwin wrote…"

Maya turned to a bookmarked page.

"Many of the views which have been advanced are highly speculative, and some no doubt will prove erroneous."[5]

Maya could see their surprise at Darwin's own admission of potential errors.

She then continued, "Let's look at how Darwin relied on faith himself. First, Darwin had faith that eventually fossils would be discovered that would support his hypothesis. He also believed that he could adequately understand the makeup of a cell. But DNA wasn't accurately mapped until 1953. Darwin based his theories on what he saw, and microscopes weren't nearly as developed as they are today. Behe illustrates his point with a bike." She turned to another page to summarize.

"Suppose a bike was a live organism going through the evolutionary process. Let's say the bike underwent enough mutations, like heavier tires, broader seats, better gears, etc. It would become more useful and the old bikes would eventually disappear from the neighborhoods."

"That makes sense," Harper said slowly, her brain processing all this new information; Jay nodded in agreement.

Maya went on, "However, as Behe imagines Darwin's theory, bikes would eventually evolve into something even more complex and powerful, like motorcycles. Under the Theory of Natural Selection, bicycles, on their own, would have to come up with a functioning motor, replace the chain with something heavier, and arrange the motor to push the wheel instead of pedals. It would have to find a source of energy to start and run the engine and a way to reproduce that was different from before. That is what Darwin was claiming happened with single cells morphing into highly complicated living animals.

"The biggest problem with the process is that all of these complex additions have to happen at once. If just an engine is added, without a heavy chain, then the whole bicycle fails to function at all. It's a fascinating theory, but as Behe points out, in practice, it's impossible.[6]

"When a fully functioning cell adds more complex chemicals and processes, this initially results in the cell, or simple animal, becoming less capable — not more. Like going from a bike to a motorcycle, this leap would require an entire reengineering of the cell, not a gradual process. And again, if 'Darwin the bicycle maker' had understood how complicated bicycles are to start with, he would have been forced to come up with a far different theory."

Jay asked if he could glance through the book, and Maya gave it to him, pointing out the pages where Behe describes the bacterial flagellum. Harper read over his shoulder. The pages explained how DNA and RNA show the intense complexity of organisms with no sign of gradual development and added to the evidence against Darwin's theories.[7]

Maya once again continued, "Remember how I said Darwin thought fossils would support his theory? Darwin understood the problem, as he stated:

> *"When we descend to details, we cannot prove that a single species has changed; nor can we prove that the supposed changes are beneficial, which is the groundwork of the theory.[8]*

"Anthropologists have found fossils of distinctly different species, and fossils within species demonstrating micro-evolution. But while some scientists claim that transitional species have been found, there is wide disbelief even among their fellow evolutionists.

One example is the writing of noted anthropologist and evolutionist Edmund Leach. He remarked in his book, *Still Missing After All These Years*:

> *"Missing links in the sequence of fossil evidence were a worry to Darwin. He felt sure they would eventually turn up, but they are still missing and seem likely to remain so.*[9]

"You see, believing in evolution requires quite a step of faith too!" Maya exclaimed.

"Macroevolution — animals evolving from one species to another — relies entirely on 'faith,' not on credible scientific evidence. They may say that I came from a monkey, but there is no fossil evidence of a species that bridges the gap between apes and man. You see, to believe that we evolved from apes without any specific evidence is quite a leap of faith."

"Why don't all scientists just believe in God then?" Harper pulled up her sleeves, sounding frustrated. "I mean, if there's all this evidence, why aren't we hearing about it? Why are they still teaching evolution instead of creation?"

"You're asking a great question. First of all, there are a growing number of scientists who do believe in an Intelligent Designer. You remember even Albert Einstein came to that conclusion. Another great example is Jennifer Wiseman, a top Astrophysicist, leading NASA scientist, and a Director at the American Association for the Advancement of Science.[10] There are many others I could name.

"They are convinced that the evidence logically leads us to believe that exceptional intelligence was behind the order and complexity of the universe. And, there are some very bright scientists, like Dr. Hugh Ross and Fazale Rana, who have contributed to building a creation model that is scientific while acknowledging the place of a Creator.[11]

"Secondly, there are many scientists who believe there is a connection between the theories of evolution and the Bible. They don't deny the existence of God and have looked for ways to observe the connection between evolution and the Biblical view of creation. They believe *God* is a rational answer for how something came from nothing." Maya hesitated before continuing.

"Recently, there have been several books written by very well-known scientists that attempt to reconcile the connection between the two primary creation points of view. There is no question that a growing number of scientists agree that God does exist and that science gives credibility to that fact."

"I'm finding that hard to believe!" Jay said leaning forward.

"Are you familiar with the Human Genome Project?" Maya asked.

"That's the government project to map the DNA of the human body, is that right?" Jay responded.

"That project was led by Francis Collins, a world-renowned chemist and geneticist. He wrote a book called *The Language of God*. I think I brought it." She dug around in her bag, pulling out a copy with more than several pages earmarked. She flipped through while talking about his life and work.

"He grew up an agnostic, then became an atheist while getting his Ph.D. in chemistry, but in medical school, his worldview began to change. He later wrote this book to explain the terms by which scientists' work can actually come alongside faith."

"Are you saying that Collins doesn't think all the advances in technology, especially his work in genetics, refute the existence of — or even need for — God?" Jay was dumbfounded that such an intelligent scientist could come to terms with believing in God.

"Well, let me give you his explanation," Maya turned to a page in the book. "He writes,

"*The God of the Bible is also the God of the genome. He can be worshipped in the cathedral or in the laboratory. His creation is majestic, awesome, intricate, and beautiful—and it cannot be at war with itself. Only we imperfect humans can start such battles. And only we can end them.*"[12]

Harper had not seen any literature in her campus library with this point of view. "I can't believe there are leading scientists in this day and age who believe in God. Do you have a list of all these books and authors? Can you give me some more references on this?"

Jay turned and stared at Harper. He could see that she was no longer satisfied with just the one-sided arguments of Dr. Meek and other professors. Then again, he wasn't sure if he still agreed with them, either, but he stifled his feelings of doubt by concluding that thinking critically of alternative possibilities was central to the methods of philosophy as a discipline.

Maya was thrilled to see their willingness to search for evidence. Their time together had sharpened her own faith and given her the desire to build her knowledge of apologetics.

"I'll be glad to help you search further. But as I've said to you guys before, some people will never be convinced, no matter how much evidence you show them. Faith is a critical ingredient in any belief system you choose, whether you're an atheist, agnostic, or Christian.

"Do you realize that even when Jesus was performing miracles in front of the crowds, many people still did not believe in him, particularly the so-called educated people of the day? He was a threat to them. He challenged their beliefs, and more importantly, their actions.

"Many scientists, like the intellectuals of Jesus' day, are far more interested in proving there is no God instead of looking for evidence of his existence. They accept many theories of their own by faith and then adamantly reject others who admit that they don't have all the answers."

"I think that's true. In my classes, it seems pretty clear my professors are trying to prove there's no God and are never willing to even entertain an open discussion about his existence," Harper observed.

Maya nodded her head, "Faith is not a foreign concept, even to people who don't believe in God, although they may not admit it. Everyone must believe in something. And most scientists are willing to place their faith in theories that are constantly changing with every new significant discovery.

Taking a Christian viewpoint, one realizes that virtually every real discovery makes a clear connection between the creation of man and the universe with our eternal God. Some scientists refuse to even consider that an Intelligent Designer could be the answer. Again, they, too, have to live by faith — faith in their own beliefs and theories on evolution."

Harper jumped in, "And you haven't even used the Bible yet. I didn't think you could do it."

"Well, the Bible is a very important book. It teaches us clearly about who God is and gives us an in-depth view of the person of Jesus. I certainly would not want to leave it out of discussions on life's important questions, but we don't have to use it to prove that God exists or that he is the best answer for how the earth and mankind were created."

"Well, there it is," Jay interrupted. He had been enjoying listening to them, but Jay was suddenly energized by a new objection. He was sure Maya had no way to defend this ancient collection of myths. "Your book of fables! Lots of people wrote books over thousands of years. What makes the Bible more important or true than other writings? Aristotle? Plato?" He was ready to take the focus off scientific shortcomings and look at "the inaccuracies of the Bible."

Maya was enthusiastic, "I'd love to look at the Bible as a historical document: is it believable or not? What if we jump on that next week?"

"Hey, do you mind if I borrow *Darwin's Black Box* for the week?" Harper asked.

"And I'd like to take a look at that *Language of God* book if you don't mind," Jay said.

"Keep them both; I'm sure I can find other copies." Maya was thankful to see their continued interest.

Searching for More

1. Can you describe evolution?

____

____

____

____

____

____

2. What evidence exists for the creation of the Universe by an Intelligent Designer?

____

____

____

____

____

3. What is the difference between the terms macroevolution and microevolution?

---

4. Other than religious beliefs, what beliefs do you have that are based on faith?

---

5. How would you compare the complexities of the universe with the complexities of a cell?

Sources for More Study

Books

- Fazale Rana, Hugh Ross, *Who Was Adam?: A Creation Model Approach to the Origin of Man* (Colorado Springs, CO: NavPress, 2005)

- Michael J. Behe, *Darwin's Black Box*, (New York, NY: Touchstone, 1996)

- Lee Strobel, *The Case for A Creator*, (Grand Rapids, MI: Zondervan, 2004)

- Francis S. Collins, *The Language of God*, (New York, NY: Free Press, 2006).

- Jennifer Wiseman, *Gutsy Girls: Strong Christian Women Who Impacted the World*, Book Four. Kindle Edition by Amy L. Sullivan

- Michael Denton, *Evolution: A Theory in Crisis*, 3rd rev. ed. Adler & Adler. 1986), p. 100.

Websites

- www.impactapologetics.com
- www.probe.org
- Answersingenesis.org
- Creation.com
- Evolutionnews.org

Podcast

Reasons to Believe — Faz Rana and Hugh Ross discuss evidence of creation

Videos/YouTube Channels

Origin of Life Challenge w/ Lee Cronin & James Tour | Evolution of Life

https://youtu.be/FdR-ZmdFOcg?si=VB_e6knpPSLkaTjo

Brandon McGuire Channel — Daily Dose of Wisdom

https://www.youtube.com/@Daily_Dose_Of_Wisdom/about

We Have Been LIED TO About The Origin Of Life: Renowned Organic Chemist Dr. James Tour

https://youtu.be/LAwwsewPxUs?si=LwD23uW7r2Nl5iN6

Ray Comfort Channel — Living Waters Evolution vs. God Uncensored

https://youtu.be/jeSxIqAYP4M?si=B-uhN-yGAMlriEaR

---

[1] Charles Darwin, *The Origin of Species and The Decent of Man* (New York, NY: Random House, Inc.).

[2] Strobel, *The Case For Faith*, 133-136

3 Ibid.

4 Charles Darwin, *The Origin of Species and The Decent of Man* (New York, NY: Random House, Inc.) 909.

5 Michael J. Behe, *Darwin's Black Box*, (New York, NY: Touchstone, 1996) 44

6 Behe, *Darwin's Black Box*, 257

7 Lee Strobel, *The Case For A Creator,* (Grand Rapids, MI: Zondervan, 2004) 278

8 Charles Darwin, *The Life and Letters of Charles Darwin*, vol. 1, p. 120. Cited at "References and Notes: Distinct Types, *In the Beginning: Compelling Evidence for the Creation and the Flood* by Walt Brown, 2008.

9 Leach E. Still Missing After All These Years. Evolution is Dead!, 2008 Accessed October 21, 2008

10 Jennifer Wiseman, *Gutsy Girls: Strong Christian Women Who Impacted the World*, Book Four. Kindle Edition by Amy L. Sullivan

11 Fazale Rana, Hugh Ross*, Who Was Adam?: A Creation Model Approach to the Origin of Man* (Colorado Springs, CO: NavPress*, 2005)*

12 Francis S. Collins, *The Language of God* (New York, NY: FreePress, 2006), 211

—6—

The Bible is Just a Collection of Stories and Myths

Jay and Harper were running a little late today. Once they arrived, though, they realized that Maya was in a hurry too.

"I thought we could include someone else today. There's a friend of mine, a professor, I'd like you to meet. He's researched this topic for decades." Maya was standing already, "Come on," she said, looking at her watch, "His office hours only last until six."

"A professor? Here at Blanchard?" Harper hesitated, confused.

"Well, this is going to be interesting!" Jay wasn't sure what Maya was up to.

Maya smiled, "I told you not everyone was against Christianity here. You just have to dig a little deeper." She led the way out of the CowZone and across the quad to Metzger

Hall, the religion and philosophy building, giving Harper a few details along the way.

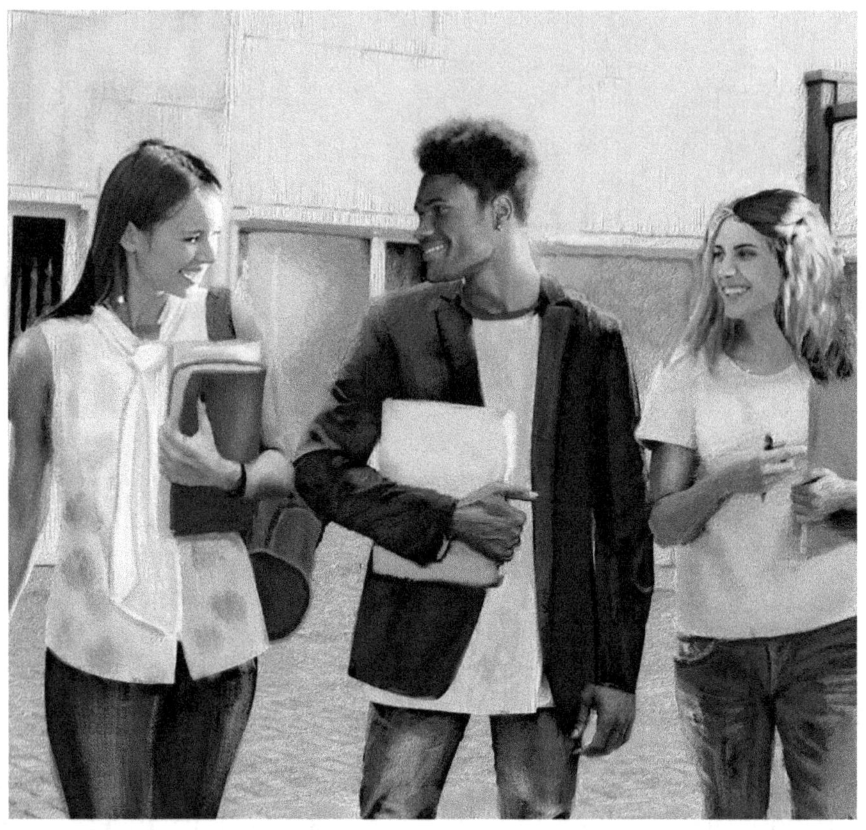

"Dr. Phillips started out as an agnostic until his best friend began asking him some powerful questions about religion. Over several years they examined a number of religions but came to believe only one had the right answers. His friend, an old drinking buddy, became a Christian first; his life changed so much that the professor became convinced himself. He will tell you that while the evidence was pretty conclusive, nothing compared to watching the change in his old friend."

"So, what does he teach here?" Harper asked.

"He teaches the New and Old Testament classes, and I think one called Ancient Texts." Jay volunteered. He knew Dr. Phillips to be a "kooky" Christian, according to some of the other professors in the department. "He used to teach an intro religion class, which I took from him when I was a freshman."

Jay had avoided him ever since; he thought Dr. Phillips was just a little too excited about religion. In contrast, Jay thought his own approach was much more reasoned.

He felt a little uneasy about going to Dr. Phillips' office, though, recalling how difficult the course was in his first semester.

"I've taken all of his courses," Maya said. "He's been a great source of information. I've been coming to him with questions I have about the Bible. He's quite a pro."

They walked up the stairs to the third floor and down the hall to a door covered in clips of cartoons. Maya knocked and a raspy voice welcomed them in.

Harper immediately noticed the professor's thick hair was completely white and his face was worn, but he had strong hands, taking each of the women's hands and eagerly shaking them. He immediately recognized Jay, gave him a wink and a smile, and shook his hand firmly as well.

"Dr. Phillips, this is Harper Forshaw, the girl I told you I've been meeting. And this is her friend Jay..." Maya was interrupted.

"Jayden Trotman, as I recall," Dr. Phillips acknowledged, breaking in. "If my ancient mind remembers correctly, you got a C+ in my 'Introduction to Religious Studies' class a few semesters ago."

Jay was a little embarrassed. And shocked that Dr. Phillips remembered him *and* his grade. Jay had implied to Harper that he'd never gotten less than an A in any class. He knew she could see his face turning red. The grade was a big reason he'd never taken another course from Dr. Phillips.

"I was still just figuring out college, I guess." Jay apologized. "You know, learning how to really study."

"Oh, I think it was one of the better scores in my class that semester." Dr. Phillips smiled and then kindly changed the subject.

"So, here we are, inquisitive minds searching for evidence!" Dr. Phillips motioned for them to sit on the leather couch against one wall and brought his creaking desk chair around to sit across from them. "So, what can I do for you scholars today?"

"Well, how do we know that the Bible is true?" Harper took the lead question. Jay was still thinking about his grade.

"You mean authenticity? How do you know that the authors of the Bible are reliable as historians?" he asked.

Harper nodded her head. "That's a good place to start."

Dr. Phillips turned to Maya, "My dear, do you remember what I told you when you asked me that same question?"

"Um, you said that the Bible claims to be the word of God," Maya started, "but it also gives us evidence to back its claims. You said that somewhere in Thessalonians it says for us to test the Bible. So, the Bible is not just giving us claims about divine inspiration, it's challenging us to prove it wrong.

And, from what you've said, no one has been able to do that." Maya said.

The professor continued, "I Thessalonians 5:21 says to 'test all things.' Harper, there are many manuscripts and doctrines that claim to have divine authority but none that have offered accurate and substantial evidence that they are true, except for the Bible. Jesus himself said to his disciples in John 14:11 that if they didn't want to believe in him, then they should 'believe on the evidence of the miracles themselves.' Even Jesus did not expect us to believe in just words, but to look for evidence."

Maya added, "I guess God wouldn't ask us to test him if he didn't think he could stand up to our skepticism."

Dr. Phillips walked over to a stack of books on his desk and grabbed a particularly large one. He turned to Jay and asked, "Can you think of any ancient documents that most archeologists and historians would consider reliable?"

"Well, I think most people would consider Plato and Homer's writings about Greek history to be accurate," Jay quickly answered, "You could certainly include the writings of the Roman historian, Tacitus. I'm sure my classics professor would say that they are very accurate."

Dr. Phillips continued. "Are you aware, my good student, that no manuscripts exist of the original writings of any of those famous men?"

"I hadn't really thought about it," Jay confessed.

"Have you ever questioned the authenticity of the translations that you've read of their philosophy and history?"

"No, but I can't say that I've ever heard a professor doubt them either. I just assumed they were accurate." Jay was uncomfortable that he hadn't thought of this before.

Dr. Phillips picked up from there, "Have you ever looked into the accuracy of the documents of the Old and New Testaments?" Jay and Harper shook their heads.

"I thought you probably hadn't, but not to worry, I've done some research for you, and others have before me. There is no document in all of ancient history with as many copies in existence as the Bible. Most historians trust the writings of history that are many times compiled three to five hundred years after the actual events.

" The earliest copies of the writings of Homer were made more than nine hundred years after his death![1] But most of the books of the Bible were written less than one hundred years after the actual events and in many cases much sooner than that." Dr. Phillips paused.

"I'm assuming you love Roman history, don't you Jayden?" he asked, turning his attention to his old student.

"Yes, I do!" Jay was glad to reference something he knew well.

Dr. Phillips continued, "Did you know the classical work of *The History of The Decline and Fall of the Roman Empire* was written in the 18th century, fifteen hundred years after the fall of Rome? Although the oldest complete copy we have of the Old Testament is about 900 A.D., we have thousands of fragments that date from around the first century or earlier."[2]

Dr. Phillips was starting to get Jay's and Harper's attention. He looked at them for a moment, allowing his facts to sink in before continuing. He turned to a page in the book he had retrieved earlier in the conversation.

"Here in Josh McDowell's book, *New Evidence That Demands a Verdict*, it tells us that, in 1948, a large number of biblical fragments were discovered in a cave in Israel. Today they are called The Dead Sea Scrolls. Those fragments date to before the second century A.D. When compared to other fragments that were both newer and younger, it was clear that the Old Testament had been meticulously copied and recopied over thousands of years, with virtually no changes whatsoever. The scribes who protected the words of the Old Testament did so almost miraculously and far beyond any other comparable documents."[3]

Jay understood the credibility of the writings, but they were still just stories to him. "So they were really good at copying things accurately, but that doesn't prove that the stories aren't myths." He shrugged his broad shoulders.

Harper agreed with Jay, "My professors said that there were so many discrepancies with archaeological finds that it's impossible to say whether or not the Bible is true."

"I believe, Harper," said the professor, "you will find that the unexplained is not necessarily unexplainable. More times than I can count, critics have claimed that what the Bible says could not be true because it doesn't make sense archaeologically, but later they found remains of a city or a site that was described in the exact way the Bible has said it would be."

"What do you mean?" Harper asked.

"Modern archaeology has continually reinforced the

historical accuracy of the Bible. As one Jewish scholar has noted, 'no archaeological discovery has ever controverted a single, properly understood biblical statement.'[4]

"Take, for instance, in Joshua chapter six in the Old Testament, the Israelites took over a city called Jericho. Do you remember how they did it?" asked Dr. Phillips.

Harper thought back to sixth grade Sunday school with Ms. Cherry and a song they used to sing. "They walked around it a few times and then blew the trumpets and 'the walls came tumbling down,'" she said, finishing with the rhythm of a song.

"Exactly!" Dr. Phillips was eager to share his research on this issue. "Historians and archaeologists alike claimed for many years that a story like that could never be true. To prove its accuracy, archaeologists would have to find a city whose walls had just collapsed for no explainable reason."

"You mean not pushed down from the outside by an army?" Maya wondered out loud.

Dr. Phillips eased back in his chair contentedly and continued, "Yes, that is correct. A British archaeologist in the 1930s discovered exactly that. He found the city of Jericho, with walls that had fallen outward, just as stated in Joshua 6:20. It would have been expected for an attacking army to push walls inward, but instead the walls were made to fall outward. At least seven other descriptions of the city were confirmed through archaeology."[5]

"Wow," Harper and Maya said in unison.

"Only the north wall was still standing. Do you know why part of the north wall was still there?"

Jay sat mystified, unable to come up with the answer.

Harper's efforts to recall were interrupted by Maya, who exclaimed, "That was Rahab's house! It was built into the wall because she helped the spies escape and God promised her he would keep her and her family safe."

Dr. Phillips enjoyed her enthusiasm. "Yes, Maya, right again. And as stated in the book of Joshua, the city was also destroyed with fire and this has also been confirmed through Jericho's many excavation projects. But these discoveries are consistent with other archeological finds as well. Again, once the details have been examined, no one has ever factually contradicted what the Bible clearly stated."[6]

Dr. Phillips continued, pulling another book from a nearby shelf, "Jeffery Sheler, a writer from *US News and World Report*, studied the issue of Scriptural accuracy in his book, *Is The Bible True?* At the very least, he concludes,

> *"The integrity of the ancient sources and of the writers and editors who drew upon them to compile the Hebrew Scriptures is not diminished by the formal anonymity that modern scholarship assigns. We may not be certain of their names, but their inspired words resonate no less powerfully as they disclose the sacred history of a covenant people and their self-revealing God."[7]*

Harper knew that Jay's brain must be in a whirl. But she also knew they had been talking only about the Old Testament. "But what about Jesus? How do we know the New Testament is true?" she ventured.

We have a similar basis of fact in believing the accuracy of the New Testament as well," Dr. Phillips responded. "Let me just mention a couple. First, most of the writers of the New

Testament were actual witnesses of the events they recorded. This is unusual because it's far more common for history writers to record events they never witnessed, events that occurred many years or even centuries earlier.

"There are more than 36,000 references to the writings of the New Testament that occur shortly after the first century A.D. One historian even stated, 'If all other sources for our knowledge of the text of the New Testament were destroyed, they would be sufficient alone for the reconstruction of practically the entire New Testament.'[8] For instance, there are the accounts of Papius, whose writings from A.D. 125 clearly stated that Mark had been extremely accurate in recording Peter's eyewitness testimony even to the point where Papius said 'there was no mistake' and 'no false statement.'[9]

"And look here." The professor stood up and went to one of his bookcases, taking a large, very dusty book off a top shelf.

"This is a collection that includes *Adversus haereses* written by a man named Irenaeus around A.D. 180. Read this," he said as both Maya and Harper leaned forward to read the yellowed page.

> *"Matthew published his own Gospel among the Hebrews, in their own tongue, when Peter and Paul were preaching the Gospel in Rome and founding the church there. At their departure, Mark, the disciple and interpreter of Peter, himself handed down to us in writing the substance of Peter's preaching. Luke, the follower of Paul, set down in a book the Gospel preached by his teacher. Then John, the disciple of the Lord, who also leaned on his breast, himself produced his Gospel while he was living at Ephesus in Asia."[10]*

"Wow." Harper sat back on the couch. "I never knew that

people had written about the Bible during that time."

"Many people aren't aware of that. But, it's important to see the evidence objectively. There is no reason to believe Papius and Irenaeus would support the writings of the New Testament unless they truly did uphold its accuracy and credibility," Dr. Phillips said.

Placing the book down on his desk, he looked at the students, "So, what's the verdict? Is the Bible true?"

Jay responded first, "I'm not totally convinced, but from what you're saying, it appears to be. I think it's just hard for some people to believe the Bible is true because it's a religious book..."

Harper interrupted, "And also, it's so hard to understand."

Jay continued with a frown on his face, "And it teaches some pretty mean stuff!"

Maya was puzzled by Jay's sudden demeanor. "Wait, what are you referring to, Jay?"

"Well, for one, how the Bible teaches Christians to hate gay people." Jay was certain of how the Bible stood on this issue.

Maya had heard this comment from some of her friends as well. Those claims had caused her to take a hard look at what the Bible says — and doesn't say — about the topic.

She sighed, "There are lots of things people claim are in the Bible that aren't really there. Would you be interested in examining what the Bible says about same-sex-attracted relationships next week?"

Jay and Harper looked at each other. Neither wanted to

be lectured on how their friends were wrong and they were now supposed to hate them.

"I'm not really sure I'm ready for a lecture on how bad gay people are," Jay murmured.

"I will promise one thing, Jay." Maya sat up for a moment with a determined look on her face. "You will not hear how much I hate my gay friends the next time we meet. We'll focus on what the Bible teaches. It may be different from what you've heard."

Harper and Jay once again looked at each other and shrugged their shoulders as if they had practiced that motion together.

"Let's give it a shot," Harper conceded. "Next time, back in the CowZone?"

"Sounds great," Maya turned to Dr. Phillips. "And thank you, Dr. Phillips! We appreciate your time."

The three students shook hands with the white-haired professor and said their goodbyes. Although Jay still thought of Dr. Phillips as a little too keen on the Bible, he no longer considered him crazy and was thankful the awkwardness about his grade was all but forgotten.

Searching for More

1. Can the Bible prove that it is true without any external evidence?

____

____

____

____

2. What evidence of the Bible's accuracy is most compelling to you?

____

____

____

____

3. Are you aware of any historical books or ancient writings other than the Bible that have a similar history of accuracy?

____

____

____

____

4. How was the Bible's accuracy preserved so precisely over thousands of years?

____

____

____

____

____

5. Is it necessary to use the Bible to prove God's existence? What other evidence would you use?

____

____

____

____

____

Sources for More Study

Books

- Lee Strobel, *The Case For Christ*, (Grand Rapids, MI: Zondervan, 1998)

- Josh McDowell, *The New Evidence That Demands a Verdict* (Nashville, TN: Nelson Publishers, 1999)

- Jeffrey Sheler, *Is the Bible True?* (New York, NY: HarperCollins, 1989)

Websites

- www.reasons.org
- www.leestrobel.com/
- www.josh.org
- www.reasonabletheology.org
- https://lifehopeandtruth.com/bible/is-the-bible-true/proof-3-history/

Videos/YouTube Channels

Brandon McGuire – Daily Dose of Wisdom

https://youtu.be/SCp2Z-uOA8Y?si=jkyli7m_rM8zI62H

The Bible is not a fairy tale – Frank Turek

Is the Bible True? Investigating the Bible

https://youtu.be/WhLtF98gNco?si=oDzSajRl8dyc9VOD

https://youtu.be/ZvQFe5uDWxk?si=uqZ85PQZPDsvtWem

TOP BIBLICAL Archeology DISCOVERIES

https://biblearchaeologyreport.com

---

[1] Josh McDowell, *The New Evidence That Demands a Verdict* (Nashville, TN: Nelson Publishers), 70.

[2] ibid. 72

[3] Ibid. 70

[4] ibid. 91

[5] ibid, 95, 382

[6] Strobel, The Case For Christ, 50

[7] Sheler, *Is the Bible True?* (New York, NY: HarperCollins,1989), 30

[8] ibid. 43

[9] Strobel, *The Case For Christ*, 24

[10] Ibid.

—7—

The Bible Teaches Hatred for the LGBT+ Community

The following week, Maya was burdened with the upcoming conversation. She'd been confused herself about the Biblical view of male and female relationships, especially when those relationships strayed outside traditional norms.

Before coming to Blanchard, Maya distantly knew a couple of high schoolers who claimed to be gay. She was very aware that her friends at Blanchard who were LGBT+ supporters clearly believed they were hated by Christians. However, when that topic came up in her home, she never heard her parents express any hatred toward the LGBT+ community.

So in her sophomore year, when one of her close friends announced she was gay, Maya began to research, not only what the Bible taught about same-sex attraction, but also other resources written by both gay-affirming Christian writers and those who espoused the traditional views more familiar to her. She spent a lot of time trying to understand what was scientifically and medically proven.

As soon as Maya sat down at their table in the Cow Zone, Jay jumped right into the topic and said, "So what does the

Bible teach? To hate anyone who doesn't believe in the old norm of a man as a husband and a woman as a wife? Am I right?"

"Jay!" Harper was startled by his loud voice, and she almost whispered. "You've got everyone looking at us! You're going to start a riot!" Harper was joking — almost.

"Sorry!" Jay was now whispering too. "But I'm a bit frustrated with people who say they 'love everyone,' " Jay lifted his fingers to mimic quotes and then continued, "but then go around preaching hate. I'm not interested in that kind of religion."

"You know, Jay, I'm not interested in that kind of religion either." Maya acknowledged.

But Jay wasn't convinced. He'd seen some of the "Christian" students on campus loudly protesting at the LGBT+ rights rallies in front of the CowZone.

"Then you've got a lot of explaining to do," he remarked with some animosity. "There was a time when I wondered if I was gay. But I certainly didn't feel like I could go to a Christian, much less a preacher, to discuss it. I knew that would be like begging for a whipping with a Bible!"

"So where did you go?" Maya asked compassionately.

"Nowhere really." Jay was remembering a day when he wondered if he had a crush on a long-time friend. "I was 15 at the time and had a very close friend, a guy. We'd been friends for many years and at times it seemed like more than just a normal friendship. I might have even said I loved him. People were talking about how it was fine for guys to like other guys, so I thought maybe Chris and I were more than just friends."

"You never told me about that," Harper said with surprise.

"That's because it never went anywhere," Jay replied.

"What happened next?' Maya was listening intently. She could see that Jay was trying to honestly describe the relationship.

"Brooke happened." A smile came across Jay's face. "Brooke moved into our neighborhood, and honestly, I kind of forgot about my friendship with Chris. I was more interested in hanging out with her than with him. In a few weeks, she was my girlfriend. And then, in a few months, she wasn't. But by then, I wasn't really thinking about Chris in that way anymore. My relationship with Brooke pretty much answered my question about whether I was gay. I guess you could say I just grew out of it, but I know that's not what happens for everyone."

"No, of course not." Maya was following his train of thought. She also knew that in middle school and most of high school, her closest friends were girls, but she most enjoyed sports and "boy" things.

"I was often called a 'tomboy' growing up. My mom played basketball when she was in high school and I wanted to be an athlete too. I certainly didn't care very much for dolls and playing house. I spent most of my time outdoors, usually playing with boys."

"I had no idea, Maya!" Harper raised her voice in surprise. "I just remember seeing you at the high school prom, and I thought you were the prettiest girl at the dance! I wanted to look just like you when I was a senior."

"You're so nice to say that, Harper. I didn't feel like I looked all that pretty that night, but I did have a lot of fun." Maya reminisced. I still like to play sports — tennis mostly — although I've never been attracted to girls other than just as normal friends. But I've often told my close girlfriends I loved them. It never seemed odd; they were just my best friends."

Harper had been listening intently. "How do you know what kind of love you have for someone?"

Maya noticed the puzzled look on Harper's face and said, "Well, let's start there, then. How would you define 'love,' and what does it mean to 'love' someone?"

Jay and Harper agreed that it would be a good place to begin. They knew that "love" could be used in many different ways.

Maya brought up a relevant example. "Hey, don't you just love these CowZone milkshakes and smoothies? That's the reason we come here, isn't it?"

Harper was immediately drawn to her butterscotch/honey milkshake. "I think I get where you're going, and yes, I just love this milkshake!"

"Yes, Maya." Jay blurted, instantly bored with this simple picture. "Not all love is the same, is it?" he deadpanned.

"There can be a big difference in meaning when we use that word, don't you agree?" She continued as Harper and Jay nodded their heads.

"If I say I love a milkshake, and I say I love my mother,

then people immediately understand I'm talking about two entirely different kinds of love. A milkshake is a preference. But I would do almost anything for my mother. I know that she loves me and has done everything she could to care for me throughout my life…hardly the same thing as love for a dessert. My mom and dad say they love each other, too, and that's another kind of love. Also, the way they behave toward each other is very different from how they treat me. And then, of course, my love for my friends is quite different, too.

"But the word 'hate' can also be used in many different ways." Maya sat up in her chair, wanting to make an important point. "We can hate certain foods or clothes or movies, but when we say we hate someone, that brings an entirely different perspective on a relationship."

"Yes it does," Harper said as if thinking out loud. She kept her voice low and looked around nervously as she was very conscious of the sensitivity of the topic at Blandard. "And sometimes you might say you 'hate someone' but what you really hate is what they're doing rather than actually hating the other person."

"Exactly!" Maya saw Harper was getting the point. "I hate it when my brother burps at the table. I hated it when my teacher criticized my poem in ninth-grade English class. I hate it when I hear people say things about my friends that I know aren't true. But what I'm hating is their behavior, not the person. I'm confident of my mom's love. But that love also includes a willingness to point out behaviors she believes are harmful — harmful to myself or others. You could say, she 'hates' those behaviors."

With some reluctance, Jay joined in. "I get it. You're saying the Bible teaches Christians —to use the phrase I've heard you guys say — 'to hate the sin, but not the sinner?' " Jay didn't sound like he agreed with the slogan.

"I see it differently," Maya said. She'd heard that phrase used too many times in church discussions, but perhaps for different reasons.

"Hating the sin and loving the sinner is often said, but too often, not done. If you're focused on hating, it's hard to show love and compassion."

"See I told you, that's why Christians hate the LGBT+ community!" Jay's emotions took over, and he was momentarily unable to keep his voice down. Harper gave him a sharp nudge with her elbow.

Maya understood why Jay felt this way.

"The hating part is easy, but the loving part, that's very difficult. But that is the real definition of love — going beyond what is thought to be possible, always with the best interest of the other person in mind, even if that means sometimes offending them — like my ninth-grade English teacher. I didn't like her for almost a full semester until I finally understood she was only trying to make me a better writer.

"What you're seeing, Jay, is how people misuse the Bible. Christians sometimes misquote the Bible, but even worse, every Christian is guilty, at times, of failing to live by it. I heard a phrase by Greg Koukl that I think captures the reality of how some Christians treat others: 'If an orchestra plays Beethoven's Fifth Symphony poorly, we don't blame Beethoven!' Some Christians don't follow the beautiful music of Christ very well, I'm afraid."

A clang rang out above the voices in another part of the sitting area. Then students started laughing as they saw that someone had bumped into a table and a tray of drinks had toppled. It was a welcome pause in the conversation.

Maya glanced down at her green notebook while Jay and Harper sat quietly, thinking deeply about all that had been said, tuning out the many conversations going on around them. They both felt a bit confused about how Christians were supposed to respond.

Maya wanted to share more about what she'd learned. "Can I refer to another Bible passage?" she asked. "I hope it will help you understand what the Bible is really teaching."

Harper and Jay were listening closely and nodded. Maya was thankful she'd kept their attention so far and that the conversation remained calm on such a hot topic at school these days.

"In the Sermon on the Mount, one of Jesus' most extensive teachings, he warns his followers to be careful about judging others.

> *"How can you think of saying to your friend, 'Let me help you get rid of that speck in your eye,' when you can't see past the log in your own eye?' "[1]*

"Ok", Harper said, "Explain, please!"

"Jesus is being very clear — in verse 5 he says,

> *"Hypocrite! First, get rid of the log in your own eye; then you will see well enough to deal with the speck in your friend's eye.*

"I point this out because what I'm going to say next is very important.

"It's true the Bible says that much of the behavior embraced by the LGBT+ community is wrong. But in almost every one of the commonly cited passages on the topic of homosexuality, the Bible equates those behaviors with other sins — like adultery, theft, lying, gossiping, cheating, idolatry — even greed."[2]

"Gossip and greed, too?" Harper was surprised.

"When Paul speaks of those sins, he tells us that Christians have been redeemed from all of them."

Maya paused for a minute to see if Harper and Jay were listening. They were looking at each other now, not quite sure how to respond.

Jay wondered out loud. "So, I think I get your points. Jesus is telling his followers to be careful when they judge others. First, you have to admit your own faults. And you're equating the actions of LGBT+ people with the wrongdoings of other people? This is what you're saying the Bible teaches?"

Maya acknowledged Jay's summary with a nod. She knew not everyone was going to agree with her point of view.

She continued, "And the Bible teaches us that we must demonstrate love if we're going to follow the example of Jesus. In I Corinthians, chapter 13, we're told that if we don't show love to those around us, we are nothing more than a 'noisy gong.' In other words, if we don't approach people in a loving way, then nothing we say will matter — it's all just noise. That doesn't mean we shouldn't say anything when someone is doing something wrong, but the Bible teaches that we must first have love for that person."

Harper now jumped in. "But my gay friends don't believe they're doing anything wrong! They say, "God made me this way. It can't be wrong if he created me like this!'"

Maya knew this argument was likely to come up and she flipped to her previous research notes on the topic of people with same-sex attraction as well as bi-sexual and transsexual claims.

"There are certainly people who claim they were made that way. And yet, there is no scientific research that supports that claim. Preston Sprinkle, in his book, *People to Be Loved: Why Homosexuality is Not Just an Issue*, quotes a study by the American Psychological Association:

> *"There is no consensus among scientists about the exact reasons that an individual develops a heterosexual, bisexual, gay, or lesbian orientation. Although much research has examined the possible genetic, hormonal, developmental, social, and cultural influences on sexual orientation, no findings have emerged that permit scientists to conclude that sexual orientation is determined by any particular factor or factors."* [3]

"Other important research points out that in studies of twins (both identical and non-identical), there is only a 'weak' connection with genetics," Maya continued.

"After reviewing the results of many different studies, the analyst concludes,

> *"'Where the development of homosexuality is concerned, twin studies have demonstrated that nurture is far more important than nature.'*

"Obviously, if same-sex attraction existed at birth, you would expect there to be a very strong correlation of sexual preferences among identical twins. Nurture seems to be a much, much stronger contributor.

"Although there's no medical research that has discovered a specific genetic link to same-sex attraction, medical research *has* found genetic links to other behavior that we as a society don't find acceptable."

"What do you mean?" Harper asked.

"Just one example is alcoholism. It's been well-known for many years that genetics contributes to alcoholism, and even to other types of addiction. However, scientists also recognize that nurture plays a role in someone becoming an alcoholic or an addict. But regardless of the contribution of genetics, addictions are not viewed as positive for society. It's often accompanied by behaviors that destroy relationships and cause negative health and economic impacts to the addicts, their families, and even their communities."

Jay was uncomfortable aligning his LGBT+ friends with alcoholics. "So, are you saying alcoholism and same-sex attraction are equally wrong?" he questioned

"Well, yes and no, Jay." Maya wanted to be clear. "I want to say again, we're all struggling with what the Bible says is sin, so I need to love everyone who is trying to deal with their behavior. That's what the Bible teaches us to do. Start with love, but don't ignore behaviors that lead to harmful things."

"Like what?" Harper chirped.

"Abigail Shrier, a research journalist, has done a lot of

work on the topic of gender dysphoria. She has made some very important points. She's also shown that much of today's claims of transsexualism are being influenced by friends, teachers, and media — especially social media. She points out a recent study in the UK that shows how claims of gender fluidity have grown 4400% among teen-age girls. She also points out that girls between the ages of 13-15 are recognized as the most easily influenced age group."[4]

"Interesting," Harper remarked pensively, remembering her own adolescent yearning for friends. "Just yesterday I was in the mall and noticed how often I saw groups of teenage girls walking along together. It was kind of weird how each different group of girls were all dressed alike. Same pants or same skirts. Same tops or sweaters. Same shoes. They all seemed to want to identify with each other. Once I noticed it, I thought it was funny every time I saw another group of young girls that were dressed alike."

Maya had noticed the same thing among groups of common-aged girls. "This immense desire to be accepted and to be easily influenced during teen years is a well-known phenomenon among researchers. The impact is clear, especially when it comes to transgender choices. And it's affecting both girls and boys alike.

"It becomes very scary when the solution for a child or teenager claiming to belong to a certain group results in premature medical intervention. Today, there are many people who only later, as older teenagers or adults, deeply regret the irreversible physical and psychological damage that occurred to them during a seemingly 'temporary' phase of their development."[5]

It was obvious to Maya that Jay and Harper were thinking through this complicated issue but were still on the fence.

"You may remember that I mentioned Rebecca McLaughlin. She was the one who wrote the book *Confronting Christianity*. What many people didn't know about her before she wrote the book is that she admits to having same-sex attraction. She also refers to a good friend of hers, Rachel, who not only toyed with same-sex attraction but had numerous encounters with females. They have both become Christians and today are happily married to men. Both of them also admit they still struggle with same-sex attraction whenever they are tempted outside of marriage. Yet they also have many friendships with other women, which they view as intimate relationships, but are not sexual at all.[6]

"You see, it's not a sentence of condemnation to have same-sex attractions, much less close personal relationships with others of both sexes. Growing up, all my close friends were other girls. But when there is a temptation to turn those relationships into a sexual encounter, regardless of the other person's gender, that's when we are called to resist sex outside of marriage. Our challenge is to not give in to those temptations."

"I've got to think more about this issue," Jay admitted. "I just know that my LGBT+ friends do not feel that the Bible or Christians are very loving toward them. I'm starting to be more open to the Bible, but I wouldn't call myself a Christian. I don't want them to think I don't care about them either."

"There would be no reason for you to reject them as friends, Jay, just because you might begin to believe the Bible is true. Jesus would not have rejected them either. He always led with love. His greatest frustrations were not expressed toward those who were on the margins of society but toward the self-righteous religious leaders of his day. This approach is one of the very reasons we know Jesus was not just 'a good teacher.' His behavior toward sinners was God-like.

"The Bible says,

"Love is from God, and whoever loves has been born of God and knows God. Anyone who does not love does not know God because God is love."[7]

Maya wanted Jay to understand just how Jesus approached people who did not feel accepted by others. His love for those who were struggling was a vitally important demonstration of who he was, as Maya believed — God in the flesh.

"That's an important issue for me to fully understand." Jay needed some time to think through their discussion today and knew they were running out of time.

"Me too," Harper was very interested in the topic of Jesus himself.

"You've said that Christians believe Jesus was more than a good teacher, right?" asked Jay, thinking about next week and a topic for discussion.

"I've even heard Christians say that Jesus was actually God. But how could that be? I understand that his teaching was helpful, but God, here in the flesh? That's a little too impossible for me to believe."

Jay just didn't see how someone in an actual body who

was walking around, eating, sleeping, and breathing could be God too. It seemed like mythology to him.

Maya smiled. "I know there's still a lot we could discuss about same-sex attraction. However, now you're talking about the most important question yet: Was Jesus just a good teacher or actually God himself? I've got a couple of books for you to read on today's topic if you want. But next week, would you like to focus on Jesus?"

"That would be awesome!" Jay was anxious to hear more about who Jesus was.

"Then next week we'll focus on examining Jesus, based on what he said about himself and what others said about him. I recently had a conversation with Dr. Phillips on Jesus. Do you mind if we meet at his office again next week?"

Jay and Harper both shook their heads. Maya pulled a few books out of her bag and handed them across the table.

The three of them walked out of the CowZone with a lot to think about. Next week could be very interesting!

Searching for More

1. What are your friends saying about same-sex attraction at school or in your neighborhood?

____

____

____

____

____

2. What kinds of sports or other activities are often shared with all your friends, regardless of their gender?

____

____

____

____

____

3. Do you feel that you are guilty of any of the sins listed in 1 Corinthians 6.9-11? In what areas do you struggle the most?

____

____

____

____

4. What are some ways that you can show love to others with whom you disagree?

____

____

____

____

5. Have you ever seen someone mistreated because they did not agree with a larger group of people? How did you respond?

____

____

____

____

Sources for More Study

Books

- Jackie Hill Perry, *Gay Girl, Good God: The Story of Who I Was, and Who God Has Always Been* (Nashville, TN: B&H Publishing Group, 2018)

- Abigail Shrier, *Irreversible Damage: The Transgender Craze Seducing Our Daughters* (Washington, D.C.: Regnery Publishing, 2020)

- Nancy Pearcey, *Love Thy Body: Answering Hard Questions about Life and Sexuality* (Grand Rapids, MI: Baker Books, 2018)

- Gregory Koukl, *Tactics* (Zondervan, 2019)

- Preston M. Sprinkle *People to Be Loved*: *Why Homosexuality Is Not Just an Issue* (Zondervan, 2015)

- Sam Alberry, *Is God Anti-Gay? And Other Questions About Homosexuality, the Bible and Same Sex Attraction* (Christian Audio and Blackstone Publishing, 2021)

- David Martin, *Rewriting Gender? You, Your Family, Transgenderism and the Gospel* (Christian Focus, 2018)

Websites

- abigailshrier.com

- Alisachilders.com

- Centerforfaith.com

Videos/YouTube Channels

What do Christians have against homosexuality? Tim Keller

https://youtu.be/nxqQag3zgp4?si=fJseZ4J_FP-89hVO

https://youtu.be/Q2G9kSUyiQI?si=1sMGlyjZ_533PqUw

A Christian Response to Pride Month - Alisa Childers with Frank Turek

---

[1] Matthew 7:4 NLT

[2] 1 Corinthians 5:9-11

[3] Preston M. Sprinkle, People to Be Loved: Why Homosexuality Is Not Just an Issue (Grand Rapids, MI: Zondervan, 2015)

[4] Abigail Shrier, Irreversible Damage: The Transgender Craze Seducing Our Daughters (Washington, D.C.: Regnery Publishing, 2020) 26

[5] ibid

[6] Rebecca McLaughlin, Confronting Christianity (Wheaton, IL, Crossway, 2019) 157-158

[7] 1 John 4:8

—8—

Jesus Was a Good Teacher, But He Wasn't God

Harper was beginning to see that many of her questions could be answered with or without the Bible. And Jay had made comments over the last couple of weeks that led her to believe that he, too, was changing his mind. She sensed that this week would be important. She'd planned to read some of the New Testament for herself before their meeting, but she never got around to it.

To Harper's and his own surprise, Jay was really enjoying the discussions with Maya. Especially after their conversation with Dr. Phillips — Jay seemed to have a new perspective.

As they walked into the CowZone to grab coffee before they met Maya for their trip to the religion building, Harper thought again about the major problems they'd discussed. She also recalled Jay's words — spoken not long after they first met — "Sunday school stories are just nice apocryphal stories about a great man, like George Washington and the cherry tree. Jesus was a great teacher, but that doesn't make him God."

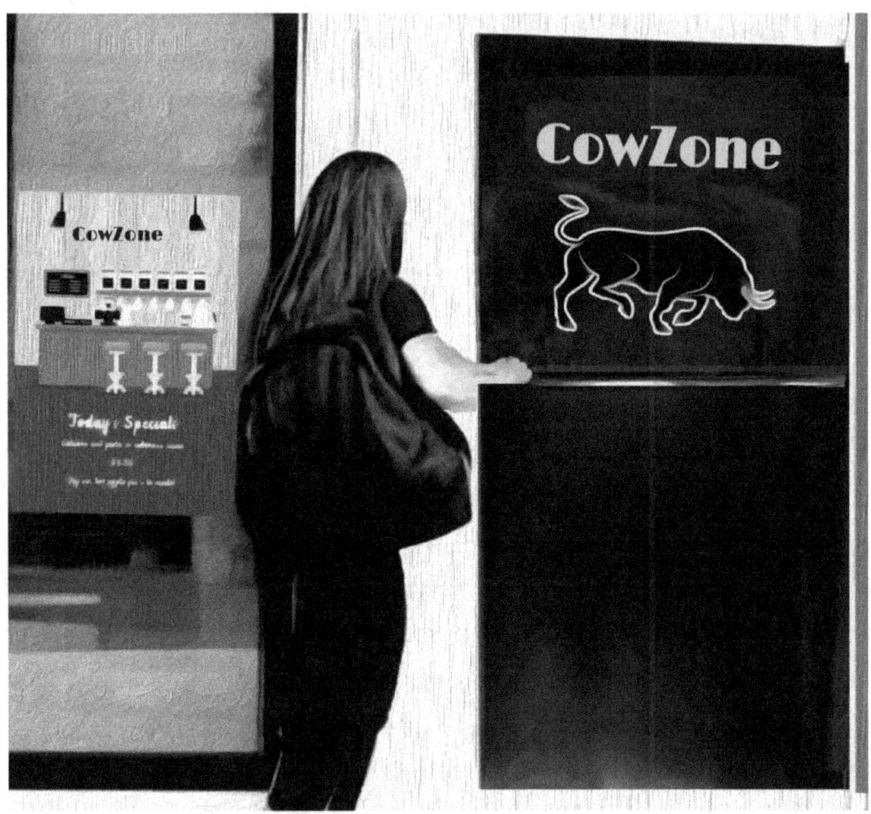

Just then, Maya walked in, breathless and looking like she'd just sprinted across campus. "Hey guys, sorry I'm late! I had to grab my teacher after class and ask her about a paper I'm working on."

She turned to Jay, "I'm so glad you could make it again, Jay."

"What's the paper on?" Harper asked, handing her a coffee as they headed toward the religion building.

Maya explained, "It's on Confucius. He was a philosopher and thinker who influenced a great deal of Eastern thought in China, Korea, Vietnam, and Japan. He wanted to change the government and the way people treated each other. His work is still very popular throughout a lot of Asia. You could say it's..."

"...kind of like Christianity. Confucius was their teacher, like Jesus was the teacher of Christianity," Jay finished.

Maya looked at him in surprise. "Well!" she said as Jay opened the door to Metzger Hall, "Let's ask Dr. Phillips what he thinks."

Jay expected he knew much more than Maya or Dr. Phillips on the subject, having done quite a bit of research on the famous Chinese philosopher and his principles. He began the discussion once they reached the small office and found their places on the couch.

"No time to lose, Dr. Phillips!" Jay sank down on the old leather couch. "We were talking about a couple of great moral teachers on the way over here, Confucius and Jesus. I think their teachings were quite similar. What do you think?"

"So Jayden, tell me what you know about Jesus," Dr. Phillip started.

"Okay, do you mean the 'Jesus' that preachers today want to make him out to be?" Jay was still very skeptical about what he knew of Christian churches. "Or what has been written about him historically?"

"Well, have you found that Confucius ever claimed to be God? Or that he ever claimed to be able to provide an afterlife for his followers?" Dr. Phillips stood up and began to search the sea of books on his shelves.

"Well, not that I can recall." Jay felt a little more challenged than he expected.

"But does that matter? Maybe like Confucius, Jesus just taught people how to live a good life. He was a good man, and a good teacher, and taught people how to live more at peace with one another. Even my philosophy professor agrees with that, and he's an atheist! Being a good person is what really matters anyway, right?" Jay was now speaking more rapidly.

Harper was almost amused, sensing she was going to learn a lot from this week's meeting. She seldom saw Jay so on edge. This was a different side of him from the cool and collected teaching assistant speaking in Philosophy 101.

Dr. Phillips replied, "Jayden, Confucius is just one example of a good teacher trying to teach social harmony. You could say some of the same things about Mohammed, Buddha, and many others whose teachings have been adopted as religions. And yes, some people certainly saw Jesus as just a good teacher even while Jesus lived. But Jesus believed and taught to those who would listen that there was much more to his life than just being a good teacher."

"I'm not sure what you mean." Jay looked confused.

Dr. Phillips now had a familiar-looking book in his hand. "Jesus also had quite a different entrance into the world from the rest of those folks."

"Oh, you mean the virgin birth myth?" Jay blurted out.

"That was certainly a different entrance, but I was referring to all the predictions about Jesus before his birth. Let me read you something from Josh McDowell's book.

"*Evidence That Demands a Verdict*?" Maya remembered the book.

"Ah, do you remember from our last discussion? Well here's the result of McDowell's study on the probability of Jesus fitting the description of the coming Messiah." Dr. Phillips flipped to the page he was looking for and glanced up for a moment to explain, "He quotes the research of a man named Stoner," then continued.

> *"Stoner considers 48 prophecies and says, 'We find the chance that any one man fulfilling all 48 prophecies to be 1 in 10^{157} … The estimated number of electrons in the universe is around 10^{79}. It should be quite evident that Jesus did not fulfill the prophecies by accident. He was who He said He was. (John 14:6).* '"[1]

Dr. Phillips looked up. "Now, who predicted the appearance of Confucius, Mohammed, Buddha, or Gandhi? And did their appearance fulfill hundreds of years of prophecy by numerous different writers?"

"I'm not aware of any evidence that their lives were predicted in advance," Jay admitted, trying hard to ignore the obvious. "But they all taught about being good and about treating others with respect and making the world a better place. How is Jesus any different in that respect?"

"Well, Jesus did preach about living a different, more

loving way of life," Dr. Phillips responded. "He spoke boldly of tending to the poor, nursing the sick, and being kind to others. He was also the first religious leader to openly proclaim the need for women to be treated equally in society. But, taking a look at the Bible, the most well-known book about Jesus' life, his life had a purpose beyond teaching people to be good. Even his death was predicted by him in advance, and that, too had a purpose: to pay the penalty of our sin so that those who believe in him might live eternally."

Jay shook his head furiously. "I knew we'd have to get to that 'sin' part. You think we are all 'sinners,' don't you?" He didn't agree with this part of Jesus' teachings.

"I think sin separates us from God, and Christianity provides an answer that's different from all other religions," Maya finally spoke. It didn't require a professor to know where Christianity stood out from all other major world religions.

But Jay was troubled with the idea of sin, "Not every religion believes that we are all sinners."

Dr. Phillips saw Jay and Harper look at each other with confidence. "No, in fact, Christianity is quite different in how sin is attributed to all individuals. But all major religions say that you must overcome your imperfections to live in an afterlife if they believe in one at all. And they all teach a required form of discipline or actions that are required before you're acceptable to their religion. But Jesus didn't teach that you could be good enough to be acceptable to God."

Jay was now confused, "I thought you just said he taught us to be good?"

"Ah," said Dr. Phillips, "there's a very important difference. Other religions teach that you must be good enough. But Jesus taught that only *He* was good enough to meet the requirements of a perfect God. What makes Christ distinct from every other so-called 'good teacher' is that he claimed to pay the ultimate price for everyone's sin. He sacrificed himself, and for that to be enough, he had to be God himself. This outrageous statement was his claim. That makes him unique from all the other 'good teachers of religion' you refer to. And he had to be more than just different. With a claim that outrageous, he had to be right."

"Yep. If someone claimed to be God, then they'd better be right. Otherwise, they'd be crazy. Or perhaps trying to deceive as many people as possible for their own personal gain." Maya paused in thought for a moment.

Harper had been listening intently, "So you're saying that Jesus actually claimed to be God? I know we talk about those things in church, but I don't think I've ever read that he claimed that he was God. I didn't think those claims were made until long after Jesus was gone." Jay nodded as she spoke.

"That's not only what Jesus said about himself, it's also consistent with the evidence he presented by his actions," Dr. Phillips suggested. "Maya, do you remember what Jesus said about himself?"

Maya recalled the time she spent last year talking with Dr. Phillips about this topic. She remembered several significant comments that Jesus made about himself.

She cited some examples, "I believe in John 10:30 he states

clearly, 'I and the Father are one.' And when he said that, the Jewish leaders immediately tried to stone him because they said he was 'making himself out to be god.'

"Another example I remember is in John 8 when Jesus uses the same phrase that God used when he told Moses his name. Jesus tells the Pharisees, 'Before Abraham was born, *I am.*' (John 8:58). And again they tried to stone him for blasphemy."

"Good memory," Dr. Phillips complimented Maya. "And others thought the same thing. He claimed on several occasions to have the very angels of God at his disposal. He also took on the name, the 'Son of Man,' the name reserved for the Messiah, the Savior of Israel. Josh McDowell points out that Jesus assumes at least 18 names that were used in the Old Testament for God, including Creator (John 1:3), Judge (Matt. 25:31-46), Shepherd (John 10:11), Forgiver of Sins (Mark 2:7, 10), Light (John 8:12), and God (John 10:28)."[2]

Dr. Phillips let all this information sink in for a minute before continuing. "But Jesus knew that words were not enough, so he suggested to his disciples that they also look at the evidence."(John 14:11)

Jay was beginning to feel overwhelmed but was impatient to keep moving. "What evidence are you referring to?"

"Let's use the analogy of a sketch artist. Lee Strobel uses it in his book, *The Case for Christ.* Have you ever heard of a sketch artist?"[3]

"They're the people who sit down with witnesses of a crime and use descriptions of the criminals to come up with an accurate picture of what they look like," Jay answered, puzzled at this analogy.

Harper spoke up, "Yeah, I'm amazed at some of the sketches that I've seen and how close they can come to drawing a picture of the actual person."

"Right," Maya said. "Strobel shows that, in the same way, the Old Testament 'sketches' a picture of God — it describes Him as omnipotent, omnipresent, and omniscient; an accurate picture of God. He's all-powerful, everywhere, and knows everything, right?" Maya made sure Harper and Jay were following her approach, and then continued, "Now if you look at the picture of Jesus in the New Testament, does he embody those same characteristics? Could we recognize Jesus as God if we knew what God looked like?" Dr. Phillips beamed at her.

"You mean, if I knew what God looked like, and Jesus looked the same, then I could recognize Jesus as God?" Jay asked, shifting uncomfortably in his chair.

"Exactly," Maya replied. "See, it's important to look at it that way because it's often a struggle for people to believe that Jesus could be present here on earth and also be God at the same time."

"Because it's like having two different sketches and trying to make them into the same person," Harper said.

"That's what it seems like. But it's only two half-sketches, and when they are put together, you can see a very clear, distinct picture of Jesus, the Son of Man and Son of God. Jesus cannot be just man or just God, he must be both."

"Okay, I kind of see what you're saying. So how can you

prove Jesus matches the sketch?" Jay was skeptical.

"Well, let's take a look at the Bible and see," Maya pulled out a worn leather Bible from her bag and flipped through the New Testament, the most vivid portrayal of Jesus' time on earth. "First we'll look at Jesus, here in Matthew 28:18. Tell me what Jesus says," Maya handed the Bible over to Harper.

Reading aloud, Harper quoted,

"All authority in heaven and on earth has been given to me."

"What do you think he's saying here?" Maya asked.

"Jesus is telling them that he has all power and control, in both heaven and earth." Harper was watching Jay consider the comparison.

"So, what characteristic of God would that be?" Jay wasn't sure.

"Omnipotence, he's all-powerful," Harper replied.

Maya continued the search. "So we have omnipotence, check. Okay now read verse 20 in that same chapter."

Harper glanced back down at the page,

"Surely I am with you always, to the very end of the age."

"Now flip over to Matthew 18:20." Maya looked over Harper's shoulder.

"Where two or three come together in my name, there am I with them."

Harper looked up.

Jay was thinking, "So he's saying he's present no matter where we are; he's omnipresent."

Maya smiled, "You're catching on pretty quickly! Okay, now, John 16:30. I have it bookmarked there, yeah. Harper, let Jay read that one."

Jay noticed immediately, "It's not Jesus talking."

"Just trust me, keep reading." Maya was familiar with the verse. Jay read,

"Now we can see that you know all things."

"It's John speaking to Jesus, confirming the third characteristic of God in him, which is what?" Maya asked quickly.

"Omniscience; Jesus was all-knowing too." Jay was thinking that this Jesus was different than what he remembered from his sporadic church attendance as a young kid.

"Exactly," said Dr. Phillips. "Jesus embodied all the characteristics of God, but he was also a human being. Hebrews 2:18 tells us that, although he was without sin, he was tempted just like we are. And there are several accounts of him weeping, of him being hungry, emotional, and even tired. Those are all human characteristics. He was a good teacher; he taught incredible sermons about good things and loved even the weakest and ugliest around him with a passion for teaching them the value they possessed outside of what the world thought of them."

"But," Harper interrupted, "You're also trying to say he wasn't just a teacher. He had all the characteristics of a good teacher but they overlapped with other ones. His attributes showed him to be God. That's what you mean." Harper glanced at Jay, wondering if he would be angry at her conclusion. Jay had stood up and was staring out the window, deep in thought.

Dr. Phillips was delighted by the way Harper was responding. "Yes. Other religions may have good teachers who show their followers supposedly good ways to live. But the truth is that Jesus was the only good teacher who claimed to be God. And very importantly, his followers not only believed that he was God while Jesus was still living, but they proclaimed that truth publicly after he had been crucified.

"And it was exactly that belief that drove them to teach about Jesus despite being persecuted — even when they were put into prison or killed.

"Could Jesus make these claims, convince his followers of the same, and still be a good teacher? If he is leading people astray, even to their own deaths, is that what a good teacher would do? Or do you think that Jesus was a liar, or at best just plain crazy? What do you think Jayden?" The old professor decided not to avoid such an important question, no matter how awkward it might be.

"I don't see how he could be so good and not tell the truth. Or how he could claim to be God and not be crazy — unless it was the truth," he answered slowly. "And seeing evidence of the prophecies predicted long before he was born, that's pretty compelling. But it goes against everything I believe. I want to be certain that he might be who he said he is, but it's going to take some time."

Harper was beginning to think that even Jay couldn't avoid seeing the truth when it was presented like that.

Is Jay Trotman really beginning to believe the Bible? Harper wondered if even he couldn't avoid seeing the truth.

"Here, I'll let you read a quote from R.C. Sproul." Dr. Phillips pulled out another book, *Reason to Believe,* and flipped through the pages to a highlighted paragraph. He gave it to Jay to read.

> *"Moses could meditate on the law; Muhammad could brandish a sword; Buddha could give personal counsel; Confucius could offer wise sayings; but none of these men was qualified to offer an atonement for the sins of the world…Christ alone is worthy of unlimited devotion and service.[4]*

"So where do we go from here?" Jay asked after a few moments, almost afraid to hear the answer. He was admittedly astonished that there were reasoned answers and rational logic behind the major beliefs of Christianity.

Maya spoke thoughtfully. "Jay I'd like to spend some time next week on what to do next. But let me ask you; are there any other significant questions that are keeping you from believing that Jesus is the unique son of God?"

"Please give me a moment," he responded. Then he turned to look at Harper. "Harper, I see now that I led you to believe that there was no credible evidence for God and that the Bible was merely a collection of ancient myths. Maybe I was wrong, and I'm sorry for ever saying people who believe in the Bible are crazy." Harper was touched by Jay's willingness to admit he might have been mistaken.

He turned back to Maya and spoke deliberately, "I'm not ready to accept all this as true just yet. I just want to think about it for a week. Can we talk again next Tuesday?

"Dr. Phillips, thank you for all your time. You have been far kinder to me than I have been over the past two years in my thoughts and comments about your 'kooky' Christianity. I hope to spend some more time with you in the future. My apologies."

Dr. Phillips stood and gave Jay a warm handshake and pressed his hand on Jay's shoulder. "Your apology is accepted, and my door is open any time."

Maya, Jay, and Harper exited the building in comfortable silence. When Jay and Harper grabbed a quick bite of dinner later that evening, Jay was not quite himself. But Harper felt a sense of peace washing over her.

Something important was happening. She couldn't put her finger on exactly what it was, but for the first time since coming to Blanchard, she was looking forward to opening her Bible that night.

Searching for More

1. Is there any evidence that Jesus' disciples believed that he was divine?

    ____

    ____

    ____

    ____

2. How would you argue against the biblical account of Jesus' virgin birth? Is there a logical defense?

    ____

    ____

    ____

    ____

3. How did Jesus' words and actions impact the lives of the disciples?

    ____

    ____

    ____

    ____

    ____

4. If Jesus was not God, but a messenger from God, is his message still as important? Why or why not?

____

____

____

____

5. Why is Jesus' resurrection important evidence of his divine nature?

____

____

____

____

Sources for More Study

Books

R.C. Sproul, *Reason To Believe* (Grand Rapids, MI: Zondervan, 1982)

Lee Strobel, *The Case For Christ*, (Grand Rapids, MI: Zondervan, 1998)

C.S. Lewis, *Mere Christianity* (New York, NY: HarperCollins Publishers, reprint 1980)

Ravi Zacharias, *Jesus Among Other Gods* (Nashville, TN: W Publishing Group, 2000)

Sean McDowell, *A Rebel's Manifesto: Choosing Truth, Real Justice, and Love Amid the Noise of Today's World* (Tyndale Elevate, 2022)

Websites

- www.reasons.org

- www.seanmcdowell.org

Videos/YouTube Channels

Dr. Gary Habermas – Southern Evangelical Seminary

https://youtu.be/wWhIVFJ4xUo?si=yDSVuNOB8sSZ-Sfw

Five Resurrection Facts that Occurred from 30-36 AD

 **J. (Jim) Warner Wallace Channel — Cold-Case Christianity: Is There Any Evidence for Jesus Outside the Bible?**

https://youtu.be/RebKd23Aaho?si=sevlJS0ThkG6UW9r

---

1 Josh McDowell, *Evidence that Demands a Verdict* (first published 1972. Revised Edition, Here's Life Publishers, San Bernardino, California, 1979)

2 Josh McDowell, *More Evidence That Demands A Verdict*, (evised edition, Here's Life Publishers, San Bernardino, California,), 133-134

3 Strobel, *The Case For Christ*, (Grand Rapids, MI: Zondervan, 1998) 155

4 R.C. Sproul, *Reason To Believe* (Grand Rapids, MI: Zondervan, 1982) 44-45

—9—

All Answers Must Be Known Before Accepting Jesus

It seemed like a very long week to Harper. Jay had only called her once and texted her a handful of times, but she really didn't feel like talking to him for some reason. They both needed time alone to think about their conversations with Maya and Dr. Phillips, on top of the academic workloads they had to juggle as the end of term approached.

For Maya, it felt like forever since their first meeting in Dr. Phillip's office. Jay especially had seemed shaken by all the evidence that was presented.

Or maybe I'm reading the situation wrong? Maya decided to just give them time to think about everything discussed and not press them for any decisions.

Jay and Harper walked into the CowZone separately, and Maya immediately sensed that they hadn't talked recently. She thought they both looked a little nervous.

"Hi, guys!" Maya was trying to keep her concerns in check. "How'd the week go?"

"It was a very different week for me," Jay spoke first. "It was almost eerie. I started to see through some of the weak arguments in my other philosophy classes that, in the past, didn't bother me. I think I shocked a few people with some of my questions. Dr. Meek even jokingly asked if I was on drugs or something."

Harper was the one who looked shocked. She couldn't imagine Jay challenging any of Dr. Meek's opinions. "What did you say?" She was very curious.

"He was talking about 20th Century philosophers like Bertrand Russell, Karl Marx, and Albert Camus and their views on pain and suffering." At first, Harper thought Jay was upset, but now he seemed mostly amused.

"I asked him if he had read the works of C.S. Lewis," Jay continued. "He said he had no intention of reading books written by an author who believed in fairy tales. I said that Lewis was a former atheist and wrote a book called *The Problem of Pain*. In it, Lewis says that pain is 'God's megaphone to rouse a deaf world.'[1] And I asked Dr. Meek what he thought about Lewis' statement. After ignoring my question, Dr. Meek suggested I find a class more suitable to the simple-minded."

Maya felt bad for Jay. "I know that Dr. Meek has been a friend to you. I hope you don't feel like your relationship with him is damaged."

"Oh, quite the opposite, actually! Don't feel bad for me. I think I finally have a real relationship with him. I now know where I truly stand with Dr. Meek. I can either think like he does or he will ridicule me. There is no in-between with him. I used to think that he was an open-minded, rational thinker. I now see things quite differently." Jay was smiling now.

"So what's different, Jay?" Harper really wanted to know.

Jay had more to tell, "I emailed Dr. Phillips after our last meeting. He recommended that if I really wanted to know who Jesus is, then I should start reading the Book of John in the New Testament. He even left a Bible for me at my desk in the TA room. I have to say that I haven't read anything so radical since the day I came to Blanchard. Jesus is truly one revolutionary guy! The way he talked to people who were intellectuals — putting them in their place — but, in a good way, I might add. And he talked to prostitutes, orphans, and widows and 'spoke their language.' I never knew that about him before."

Maya was dumbfounded. "Wow, Jay! I'm really proud of you. Reading the Bible! And how you've been willing to think through all these issues with an open mind."

"Well, that's just it, Maya. I can't really say that I had an open mind at the beginning. Honestly, I thought I was going to show you how smart I was and how naïve and gullible your thinking was. I was even excited about the idea of proving Dr. Phillips wrong because he was so, so religious. But my arguments were weak compared to yours. It was probably my embarrassment that kept me coming back, thinking I'd prove you wrong the next time. But this past week especially, my views of Christianity — and Christians — began to change."

Harper had been holding back her own enthusiasm, but now she felt like she could speak freely. "Same here. I have definitely been thinking differently lately. It started a few weeks ago for me." Maya could see that Harper was a changed person from the one she'd met in the CowZone that very first Tuesday.

Harper continued her thoughts, "I meant to text and tell you — I had a long conversation with my mom. I told her how I'd been behaving since I've been at Blanchard. I didn't realize that she and Dad didn't become Christians until after they left college. They too really questioned God and religion when they were in college. It was only after their marriage became a struggle that they realized life was more than just acquiring meaningless facts. She described their beliefs in college as 'empty cardboard boxes stacked on top of each other, ready to topple over at any time.'

"I guess I was beginning my own stack of boxes. Last weekend I actually went home to be with them. We prayed together for the first time in a long time. And I think I'm ready to start a serious study of the Bible. I'd like my life to be renewed in a way that I know only Christ can."

Jay wasn't aware that Harper had gone home and he was curious. "Harper, I thought you said that you weren't sure if Jesus was the only way to heaven and that you needed to know more first."

"Yes, that's partly true. I do have a lot of questions that aren't answered, Jay. Is Jesus the only way to heaven? Did he really rise from the dead? How did the virgin birth happen? Why doesn't the Bible talk about dinosaurs? What about all the genocide in the Old Testament? I still have lots of questions. But I've also come to realize that everyone must have faith in something. I want to put faith in the most reasonable, provable something — or someone. And I believe that our last eight weeks together have shown me — more than anything else — that God is real and His son Jesus is the solution for my sins."

"I'm still struggling with some of those questions. Especially the sin part," Jay admitted. "I want to say the things you've just said, but I'm not sure I'm ready."

Maya had been listening to their stories. She was very

excited to hear their words, but she was also cautious. "I want you both to know that I also have many questions, even still. There are times when I struggle with the very questions we talked about. And most of the time, I think the answers seem very clear, but then something happens to make me doubt. But I do agree with Harper; I think I've found the best answers to all the most important questions. Who is the author of the universe, and who is best to trust with my life? I believe that the rest of the answers will come. And I'm willing to seek them out and find them. So far, I've not been disappointed."

Jay turned to Harper. "Harper, I'm sorry again for making you think religion was stupid. I'd like to join that Bible Study you were talking about if you'll let me."

Harper was laughing, "Well you'll have to ask Maya. She and I plan to start it next Tuesday. And guess what? My roommate is going to join us. It seems that meditation hasn't been the answer that she thought it was going to be. She's already seen a change in me and wants to explore the Bible. Maybe your roommate would join us too!"

Maya was ecstatic, "Of course, you can join us. We'll search for even more proof AND — since we've spent the last eight weeks looking for 'proof,' maybe now it's time to find 'faith!' So invite anyone else who would like to come!"

Searching for More

1. Do you know any evidence for God – outside of the Bible?

   ____

   ____

   ____

   ____

2. Have you ever questioned whether God really exists?
    What gave you the confidence to put your faith in Him?

   ____

   ____

   ____

   ____

3. Did the prophets of the Bible base their belief on faith or
    evidence?

   ____

   ____

   ____

   ____

4. In what way are science and religious beliefs the same?

____

____

____

____

5. How are they different?

____

____

____

____

Sources for More Study

Books

- Dr. Norman Geisler, Ronald M. Brooks, *Come, Let Us Reason: An Introduction to Logical Thinking* (Baker Book House, 1990)

- S. Morris Engel, *With Good Reason* (New York, NY, St. Martin's Press, 1994)

- William L. Craig, *Hard Questions, Real Answers* (Wheaton, IL: Crossway Books, 2003)

Websites

- www.crossexamined.org
- www.christianity.com
- www.reasonablefaith.org

Podcasts

- **The Dig Bible Podcast** ("dig" into the scriptures, interviews with various authors, and topical studies of the Bible)

- **BibleProject** (In-depth conversations about the Bible and theology, podcast companion to BibleProject videos found at www.bibleproject.com)

Videos/YouTube Channels

How is Christianity different from other religions? **John Lennox Channel — Abiding Life**

https://youtu.be/pLIbg49PbHk?si=OZ2ItCIv-oPvGad0

Are Theists the Only People Who Have the "Burden of Proof?" **Cold Case Christianity**

https://youtu.be/OpPsgbOzS3A?si=ZftgyoV8REEg0w7o

Ray Comfort Channel — Just Witnessing

https://youtu.be/9LztPWytmew?si=qXyHTD3n27jOHakD

What to do to be saved

---

[1] C.S. Lewis, *The Problem of Pain* (HarperOne; Revised ed. Edition, April 28, 2015) 93.

If you enjoyed *Searching for Proof and Faith*, please

leave a review at your

favorite book retailer's website.

Thank you!